LADY YESTERDAY

Amos Walker Mysteries

MOTOR CITY BLUE · ANGEL EYES · THE MIDNIGHT MAN
THE GLASS HIGHWAY · SUGARTOWN · EVERY BRILLIANT EYE
LADY YESTERDAY

AN AMOS WALKER MYSTERY

LADY YESTERDAY

Loren D. Estleman

Houghton Mifflin Company BOSTON 1987

Cop. 2

4-87 BA 1500

Library of Congress Cataloging-in-Publication Data

Estleman, Loren D.
Lady yesterday.

(An Amos Walker mystery)
I. Title.   II. Series.
PS3555.S84L3   1987   813'.54   86-27447
ISBN 0-395-41072-X

Printed in the United States of America

S 10 9 8 7 6 5 4 3 2 1

To
TOM SULLIVAN,
the wizard in the corner

Ah, those were the days — top and bottom, breakfast dances, and real jam sessions. Let's pause here and pay tribute to Willie "The Lion" Smith, Stephen "The Beetle" Henderson, James P. Johnson, and Willie "The Tiger" Gant.

— Rex Stewart

LADY YESTERDAY

1

It was February by the time I caught up with Clara Rainey, at the end of a trail that wound to Miami and back north to a steakhouse called Astaire's in Quakertown south of Bloomfield.

The place was a long way from rock bottom. The neon sign on the roof was a top hat. Double doors that looked like big chocolate bars with the letter *A* carved on them in script led into the bar or the restaurant, depending upon which one you took. Inside, on a thick red carpet with black flocking, a group of senior citizens in high-belted suits and print dresses and strings of colored stones waited for a six-foot champagne blonde behind the reservation stand to seat them. Waitresses dressed in sky-blue tops with puffed sleeves and short black skirts slit to the ceiling breezed through the dining room carrying platters to and from the kitchen, drawing cooking smells and clatter out into the room in the current of the swinging doors. Candles sparkled in thick orange glasses on the tables and the place smelled of starched linen and leather upholstery and tip money. It was all engineered to make you hungry enough to try Astaire's World Famous Prime Rib.

At the bar I paid twice the usual amount for a tall Scotch

because the entertainment had started and carried it through an arch to the piano and set it on the glass top. Clara went on tinkering with "I Love You Just the Way You Are" and didn't look up.

She had changed her hair—it was a frosty color now, chopped off at the nape and blown out into a porch roof over her forehead—but her face was the same pale moon under the make-up and her eyes were set far apart. She had lost some weight and looked almost trim in a green satin dress with a scoop front that exposed the heart-shaped birthmark her husband had made me aware of high on her right breast. No jewelry, not even a wedding band. She was forty-two and looked it, but not in a bad way.

When she asked me for my request I poked one of my cards into her tip glass face-out and said, "Axel says to play 'Clara, Won't You Please Come Home.' "

She didn't jump up and run away. She didn't even drop a chord. Instead she took up the melody with her left hand and raised her right to test the porch roof over her eyes. For a space I wondered if I had the right party. "I thought someone would be around before this," she said then.

"I lost you for two weeks in Atlanta. I had to bribe an acting desk sergeant for a blotter item that should have been public record."

"Risky."

"Not in Georgia."

"Was he small, with glasses?"

I said that sounded like him. She made a croaking noise. "The little bastard had me strip-searched in a room with a trick mirror. I threatened to go to his lieutenant and he couldn't erase my name fast enough."

"Rough trip home."

She went on playing. "The best things in life are free, on a full stomach."

I assumed a listening attitude with my drink in hand

and she told me the story. She had run away with her husband Axel's accountant to Florida, where he'd ditched her, sticking her with the hotel bill. To pay it she'd hustled drinks in a dive called the Gold Coast Lounge, got busted with the owners when DEA took it down for trafficking in the rest rooms, was released, and hitchhiked back to Detroit, getting arrested for that once in Atlanta. In between she'd hooked a little to eat, operated a cash register in a Memphis diner, found Christ, lost Him again, and got raped by a goofed-up college freshman on his way back from Lauderdale. Reaching Michigan finally she'd drawn on three years of concert piano in high school and Darryl Astaire's weakness for ice-blondes to land this spot. She'd been away from home eight months.

I knew some of it and could guess the rest, but I let her tell it all, shaking my head on cue and sipping from my glass. She had let the Dutch boy go; it was all gushing forth now. It wasn't my business, but I liked the husky sound of her voice and the way her short strong fingers waltzed over the keys as she spoke. She played "Penny Lane" while talking about her husband and I made comments in the expected places and then we agreed that she was better off where she was. She had an apartment on Grand River and some money in the bank and something going with Astaire and when she bent her lips to smile it looked real, not the I'm-hanging-on-by-my-fingers grin in the snapshot in my shirt pocket. When I said I'd have to report to Axel Rainey she rolled her shoulders and said she'd been thinking of calling him and telling him where things stood.

From start to finish I knew everything that was coming in the conversation, including some of the phrases and the places where she would stop to wipe her eyes, complaining about all the smoke in the room. The work was getting to be like licking stamps eight hours a day and I was doing some hanging on of my own.

"Will you give me twenty-four hours to talk to him my-self?" she asked. "If he comes storming in here the way he usually does things Darryl will break his back."

"I just won't charge him for the extra day."

"Thanks." She noodled the keys. "You're sort of human for a bloodhound."

"If you run again I'll trace you again and he'll pay me for that."

"Yeah, you're hard as hell."

I passed that one up. Either my veneer was peeling or she'd learned a lot since Miami.

She shuffled her music sheets. "*There's* someone who needs a detective."

I followed the incline of her head and looked at a woman in an eggshell dress sitting at a small table by a partition with a fern hanging over it. The fern was working on dipping a tendril into her teacup and I couldn't see her face for the brass pot. Her slim hand resting on the table-cloth was an even light brown with a ring on it.

"She's been here two nights waiting to talk to Darryl. She won't say why. I told her he's out of town but she probably thinks I'm covering for him. She's in trouble. I guess I know that look."

"I've got all I need."

"It shows."

The woman turned in her chair to nail a passing waitress and I saw her face. Under a turban the same gray-white as her dress she had a profile like an Egyptian princess in the days before the Europeans stumbled in and gummed up the bloodlines, and in the candlelight her skin was the color of antique gold. Her eyes were just a little too large and her chin came just a little too close to a point. She was the best-looking feature in the room. I knew her, of course.

"Mr. Walker?"

I looked at Clara Rainey. She wasn't playing. The light

J

over the piano struck sparks off the glitter-dust on her eyelids.

"I asked if you had a request."

After a beat I scraped a dollar bill off the inside of my wallet and stuffed it into her glass. " 'Dark Lady.' " I picked up my own glass again and took it to the table.

2

"Furthermore, Iris," I said, sitting down.

It took her a moment. She was about to call someone to sweep me out the door. She'd dealt with her share of uninvited males. Her eyes got bigger than eyes have a right to get. A gold pin shaped like a unicorn with a diamond horn flickered on her turban. "Amos?"

"I like the pin. I'm not sure yet about the towel. I keep wanting to complain about the price of gas."

Her expression completed a tight 360 from anger to surprise to joy to suspicion; the old triple play. "Did you follow me here?" Her hand was resting on a white leather purse on the table with the clasp open and her fingers curled inside. I ignored it for the time being.

"Where from, Jamaica?"

She relaxed a little, but the hand stayed where it was. "I left the island a week ago. What are you here, a bouncer? Give up Sherlocking to roust the colored folks out of genteel establishments?"

Her West Indies accent had become more pronounced in her time away. I drained the glass and set it down. "Excuse it, please. I thought I saw an old friend. My mistake." I started to push myself up.

"Wait. I'm sorry."

I sat back.

"My mother died Thanksgiving Day," she said. "Not that Thanksgiving's celebrated there, but it always seems to happen around a holiday."

"I'm sorry."

She smiled. It changed everything about her. She took her hand off the purse then and ran a gold-nailed finger around the edge of her teacup. A simple enough gesture, but with as much sex in it as I'd seen her put into anything, and she'd walked past me stark naked the first time I'd laid eyes on her, in a John R whorehouse that had since been turned into a hotel for women; hotels for men being discriminatory. At the time I'd been looking for a missing woman. I was starting to think I was in a rut.

"I keep thinking about that heart pendant you got back for me, the one I was afraid to go home without because it was a present from my mother. I was pretty innocent."

"As innocent as a hooker with a heroin habit gets."

"What's sex and dope got to do with knowing the score?" Anger again.

"Not a damn thing."

"We're not getting off to the right start, are we?"

I shook out a Winston, just to be doing something. A pale brunette in a cinnamon business suit seated at the next table glared at me over her vegetable curry. We were in the nonsmoking section. I winked at her and stuck the cigarette in my mouth and didn't light it.

"People die," I said. "Living is fatal."

"Bullshit."

I didn't like it much either.

"Whoever said death is part of life just made it worse," she said. "It isn't natural at all. Talking to someone you love who's dying and them answering. Both of you knowing it and not talking about it and the world doesn't stop or even slow down like it doesn't mean nothing. We're all of us nothing and that's the score."

"Doesn't sound like we're winning."

She drank from the cup. "Bet you missed these conversations."

"You look good."

"You too. Older."

"You always said I looked older than I was."

"It's still true. I sent you a card one Christmas."

"I never answer them. Pretty soon you're trading cards with Andy and Mabel in Milwaukee and you never met them or anyone who knew them. It can make you crazy."

A waitress came around finally. Iris wasn't eating. I ordered a steak sandwich and fries and another drink for myself and the girl wrote it all down, pink tongue caught in the corner of her mouth, checked her spelling, and bounced off. She had a little white scar on the inside of her left thigh. The pale brunette was still watching me and my cold cigarette and now she'd directed her companion's attention my way. He had a graying brush cut and square black glasses and a spare chin folded over the maroon satin knot of his necktie. He looked at me, then at the food on his plate, then at me again out of the side of his glasses. He was hovering between hoping his date would forget about me and hoping I would go away.

"Lady at the piano says you want to see the owner," I said to Iris.

"She's laying him. You can always tell."

"Shame on them. Fornicating this close to Detroit."

Iris refilled her cup from the stainless steel pot on the table. "Women know what I am. What I was. I can't hide it. They get protective."

"Not that woman."

"Maybe not. Sometimes I think I might as well be wearing a scarlet letter."

_____

8

"Hawthorne didn't know anything about women."

"My father worked here four years back," she said. "It was a pancake house then."

"I thought your father died a long time ago."

"My mother's husband died when I was eleven. My father's still breathing, or was four years ago when he washed dishes here."

"Huh."

"I found my mother's wedding license and my birth certificate in an old letter box where she kept her papers. Who looks at their birth certificate until they need it? It seems I was born four months after they were married. The name wasn't my father's; not the name of the man I always thought was my father."

"Why are you looking for him?"

"Who said I was?"

I grinned. It got another smile out of her.

"Okay, I want to know what came before. Maybe I wouldn't have if I found out while my mother was still alive. Now it's important, don't ask me why. Beginnings and endings, they go together. I want to know what sort of man he was and why he didn't marry my mother."

"Maybe he didn't know."

"I want to hear him say it."

"How'd you know to look here?"

She reached inside her purse and laid a color photograph in front of me, printed on glazed paper. It showed a black man who looked a lot like Nat King Cole, straightened hair and neon grin, with one arm around the waist of a good-looking young black woman in a yellow dress standing in front of a cement block building with the letters OOL showing on a sign over the door. The first part of the sign wasn't in the picture. The man had on a white sack coat over black pants and a green bow tie on a pink shirt and he was holding a slide trombone with his free hand, the instrument resting along his forearm. I saw the family resemblance in the woman's face. She looked happy, the way people look happy in pictures taken more than thirty years ago and somehow don't in pictures taken last week. The man and woman were the same height.

"You didn't get your looks from your father."

"That's a compliment. My mother was a beautiful woman. The picture was taken in front of the old Piano Stool in Kingston. All the greats played there, Louis and Miles and Thelonius and the Duke and the Count. They tore it down when I was little to put up a roller rink. But the man who owned the Piano Stool is still alive and I showed him the picture and he said he didn't need to see it, he remembered Little Georgie Favor and his Moonlighters. He booked them out of Detroit for a weekend and held them over six weeks."

"George Favor was his name?"

"It's the name on my birth certificate. They probably met in the club. My mother used to sing a little. Her voice didn't match her looks so she got out. Videos hadn't been invented then." She drank some tea. "The old guy saw them together but he didn't mix in with performers' lives. He didn't know nothing about Favor's past or where he went after he left the island."

"Try the Chord Progression?"

"First place I checked when I got back here. They didn't know from Georgie Favor. They're into fusion now and he was Chicago Style. But someone there referred me to Josephus Wooding. He was a headliner there for a dozen years back in the fifties and early sixties."

"Joe Wooding, sure," I said. "He's alive?"

"If you can call it that. He's sick and living in a trailer behind his house in Westland. Closed the place up when his wife left him two years ago and hasn't set foot inside it since. He didn't want to talk to me, but Favor's name got me in. He said he saw my father coming out the back door of this place about four years back. Took Wooding a minute to recognize him, he'd aged that much since they shared a bill. They talked a little, told each other what they were doing, promised to get together and never did. That's as much as he knew, or was willing to tell. He shut down when I pressed him. I don't think he trusts women these days, or anyone else, but especially he doesn't trust women. He's a bitter man. Sits there all day long with a big pistol next to him. He was broken into not too long ago, they slapped him around and tied him up and took his TV and fiddle."

"What's his address in Westland?"

She gave me a number on Venoy. I got out my notebook and wrote it down. My steak sandwich came and Iris waited until the girl went away.

"I can't afford to hire you. Burying my mother and coming here took almost my last cent. If I don't find paying work soon it's back to the business bed for me."

"Welcome home present. Where are you staying?"

"Place called Mary M's on St. Antoine. It's a halfway house for working girls looking to quit. A friend of mine runs it."

I wrote it down and flipped shut the book. "You got paper on that iron in your purse? CCW is a thirty-day pop mandatory in this town."

She made as if to touch the clasp, then let her hand drop. "Eight hundred murders here last year, Mr. Detective. I'd rather face the bench than a slab."

"It's not my business unless you say it is."

"Then I guess it's not your business."

"Would the ring be?"

She glanced down at the little diamond on the ring finger of her left hand. It was mounted in a plain spider-thin

---

II

gold setting. "He's a good man. He runs a one-boat charter fishing business out of Port Royal. We're going to be married in May."

"He can't help out with money?"

"I wouldn't ask him. He thinks I'm here visiting relatives. Which I guess I am if I find one."

"I'm glad he's a good man."

"They're a long time between."

I didn't chase it. I parked the cigarette behind my right ear and constructed the sandwich from the tomato slices and lettuce on the side. The pale brunette lunged across the table she shared with the brush cut, mouth moving, and the brush cut tossed down his napkin and got up and came over. He was bigger and harder than he looked sitting down. The fat was just inertia.

"Excuse me, but are you planning to smoke that cigarette?"

I sat back, looking up at him. "Eventually."

"Could I borrow one? I left mine at home."

After a pause I produced the pack and tapped one partway out and held it up for him to take. I struck a match and he leaned down for me to light it.

"Nonsmokers," he said, straightening. "We don't interrupt their meals asking them to not smoke."

"You'd think outliving us would be enough."

He moved his big shoulders and nodded to Iris and returned to his table trailing clouds. The brunette left shortly afterward. The brush cut put out the smoke then and finished his meal at a leisurely pace.

3

Westland is a workingman's community, functional if it's nothing else, and nothing else is exactly what it is. No restaurants of note, liquor stores with iron bars that fold over the windows at closing, pool tables and shuffleboard games in bars where the customers wear Hawaiian shirts and knock back boilermakers and play Waylon Jennings and Merle Haggard on the jukeboxes. Bleak streets lined with bleak houses spreading out from the General Motors assembly plant, making a town as flat and gray as a concrete slab. We had had a lot of snow that month and it lay in rusty piles against the curbs under a battleship sky. In that season it looked like the kind of place where laid-off line workers massacre their whole families and then shoot themselves.

I had offered Iris a ride home the night before, but she had borrowed a car, and I had caught my first full night's sleep in a while and showered and shaved as if I were going someplace where they noticed such things. These days I was driving a new two-tone blue Chevy Cavalier, thanks to a bonus from a downtown legal firm whose client I'd cleared of a manslaughter charge. The interior still smelled like a plastic raincoat but the fuel injection and front-wheel drive were pleasant surprises. I hoped they lasted as long as the payments.

Sweet Joe Wooding, as he was billed in the days when the Chord Progression on Livernois presented Harry James and Benny Carter to standing-room-only crowds in dinner jackets and pink chiffon, lived, or had lived, in a one-story yellow brick house on Venoy with attached garage and overgrown hedges on either side and a paved driveway he shared with his neighbor to the right. The place had a vacant look now, like an idiot's face, and paint was curling away like dead skin from the wooden window frames. I parked in the shoveled driveway next to an exhausted-looking AMC Pacer belonging to the house next door. Some kids were building a snowman in that yard, making plenty of noise, and on the other side a fat boy in glasses and a red snowsuit was trying to coax some momentum out of an orange plastic saucer on a fifteen-degree slope. He bounced up and down and the saucer just sat there and flapped. His cheeks were as bright as Christmas bulbs.

I peered through the dusty window into Wooding's garage. No car. From the way the tools and junk were distributed on the concrete floor there hadn't been a car for some time. I didn't go to the door of the house. Instead I followed a shoveled path around to the back, where an old black man in a Russian hat and a dirty gray quilted coat was removing snow from in front of a sixteen-foot robin's-egg-blue house trailer with a television antenna on the roof.

I hesitated. It all reminded me of something. I thought of a big shaven-headed black man standing with a snow shovel in front of a house on John R, where I'd first met Iris. I thought of a house trailer in another place where Iris and I had gotten better acquainted. I was doing a lot of remembering lately. I resumed walking.

"Josephus Wooding?"

He went on shoveling with his back to me. I said it louder.

"I hears you." He got a medium load on the blade and put his back into it and threw it two feet to the side. He paused to rest.

"My name's Amos Walker. I'm looking for Little Georgie Favor. His daughter hired me."

"Man's name was George. You call him Little Georgie he go upside your head with his horn case. That shit was just for the bill."

"Like Sweet Joe?"

"No, my first wife called me that." He threw some more snow and turned around to face me, leaning on the handle. His complexion was deepwater-black under a skin of sweat and his features were laid in rectangular blocks, the forehead resting horizontally on the vertical pillars of his cheeks with the lower jaw providing a footing and the flat nose doing keystone duty. He had a thin moustache that looked dyed and his eyes were white under the irises so that he seemed to be looking up from under his fur hat. "George's girl sent you?"

I held out a card.

He went on looking at me. "Man, anyone can get one of them printed."

I produced the folder with my picture ID and the county buzzer I wasn't supposed to have. They were a little harder to get, but not very much. Anyway he nodded.

"Now I'm waiting on a reason I got anything more to say to you than I said to the girl."

"Maybe because her father left her mother like your last wife left you," I said, "and you both want to know why."

The shovel blade came up very fast and knocked my hat crooked while I was getting under it. I kept going and grasped the handle in both hands and twirled it out of his grip while he was still following through. He sat down in the snow.

I stuck out my hand and he looked at it a moment,

breathing heavily, before he took it. He came up more easily than I was braced for. He didn't weigh a whole lot more than the shovel. I gave it back to him to lean on.

I said, "My wife left me after three years. For a long time I thought it was my fault."

"It *was* my fault."

He was still panting when he turned his back on me and started toward the trailer, using the shovel like a cane. After a moment I followed.

He stood the shovel in the snow next to a set of wooden steps and we climbed them into a living room setup with an orange recliner-rocker gone grimy on the arms and a blue vinyl child's-size sofa with metallic tape smoothed over the places where the vinyl had split and a new oval rug and a small painted bookcase containing magazines and a few thumb-smeared paperbacks. There were a sink and a two-burner stove with a built-in refrigerator at one end of the trailer and a heavy russet curtain at the other, behind which would be a bed and tub and toilet. The place was old-bachelor neat without pictures or anything to indicate that the man living there was a musician, retired or otherwise.

Except for the marijuana smell that permeated the place like disinfectant in a public restroom.

The air inside felt chillier than outdoors. He took off his hat and coat and hung them on a peg next to the door and kicked a tin furnace set into the wall near the curtain. It cut in with a wheeze and a clatter of bent fan blades.

Without his coat, the architectural effect was lost. He was thin to emaciation. He was several sizes too small for his colorless shirt and old striped suitpants and the end of his narrow belt turned out, as if he'd had to make a new hole farther in. By contrast, his head with its thinning coil of black hair — it had to be dyed — looked huge. Whatever was killing him hadn't wasted its way up past his neck. Nor had it affected his balance, or the big Ruger he wore hung on his right hip would have pulled him over when he kicked the furnace. It had a six-inch barrel in a stiff black leather clip and a slick walnut handle with indentations for the fingers and had to have set him back a month's Social Security.

He saw me looking at it and smiled for the first time, showing pink gums. He was breathing almost normally now. "Fanny." He patted the weapon. "Named her for my second wife. You looked friendly enough coming around the house or I'd of knocked you down like a baby seal."

"At close range the shovel's better."

"What I thought, but I ain't got the muscle for more than one swing. I did last month. I don't want to think about March, if I see March. I got it, son. It's got me. I never thought it would, somehow."

"Seen a doctor?"

"Seen two. They wanted to admit me, shoot me full of nuke juice and go to cutting on me like an apple with a brown spot. Shit. She tell you they robbed me?"

"The doctors?"

"Well, them too. These sonsabitches roughed me over and tied me up and took my axe. Only thing I carried out of the house when Henrietta upped and left. That was my third wife. They got my TV too, but the hell with that. That bass sang sweet as Mister B."

"They get in the house?"

"No, they heard a siren and cut out. I see them again they's two dead niggers."

"Easier to talk about than carry off," I said. "Or to get along with when it's done."

"I won't have to get along with it long." He dropped into the recliner, hard enough to splay his legs. The chair dwarfed him. He hadn't the leverage to tilt it back. "George Favor. Yes, that boy blowed good tailgate. Not great; I blowed some of it myself when they wasn't no bass work and I showed him some licks he never heard of. We all of us doubled back then, not like now. I tripled on the box. What Georgie was was dependable. He was always straight and he never stepped on a man's solo. Couldn't run a band for shit, though, and it roont him."

"Ruined him how?" I sat on the sofa.

"Man, you gots to be a ripe son of a bitch to lead a band. Tommy, Jimmy, Mister Miller—Hitler didn't have nothing on them white boys. Georgie, he wanted everybody to like him. Nobody came to rehearsal twice in a row because he didn't fall on them like a safe when they didn't and they sounded like Canadian geese up there. Hell, they'd probably be a hit these days. Back then no place'd book them after a while and when George couldn't pay them they took their horns and split. He never got over it, Georgie didn't. Was all he talked about. He was solo by the time I knowed him and I never seen that big grin that was on all his pictures."

"He had it in Jamaica. They held the band over six weeks."

"Floyd Gleaner was probably still with him then. Played cornet and French horn and done the arranging and I hear he was son of a bitch enough for the both of them. He quit to work in pictures."

I wrote down the name. "Know where I can reach him?"

"Forest Lawn. Blowed his brains out through that horn twenty years back and throwed hisself under a truck in LA."

I crossed it out. "Iris says you saw Favor four years ago."

"Just about that. Harold's Hotcake Hacienda it was then. I was still driving then, parked my crate around back. When I come out after breakfast there he was emptying cans into the dumpster. I almost didn't know him. Bald, and what he had was pure white—and him we didn't call

Blackie on account of his skin, like black patent leather that pomp was, oh my, with enough straightener in it to take the bends out of the Mississippi. 'George?' I says. 'George Favor?' And he looks at me but he don't know me, but I can see now it's him all right and I says, 'Joe Wooding,' and he still don't know, but he says, 'Oh, sure,' like you do. I axed him was he working there, like he ain't got on a apron that says kitchen help all over it. He says yeah, washing dishes and cleaning up. Well, he don't look too ashamed, so I axed him was he still playing and he said he sat in sometimes at the Kitchen."

"Down in the warehouse district?"

"Man, you know another Kitchen? Well, I went down there oncet or twicet after that but I never seen him and the waiters never heard of him, so I figure he just told me that so's I didn't think cleanup's all he's good for."

"You go back to Harold's?"

He shook his blocky head slowly. "They closed it not too long after and then someone turned it into the kind of place you got to scrub your nails and put on a clean shirt before they let you in the door. Henrietta cut out about that time and who gives a shit about Georgie Favor."

I did some scribbling. His eyes were burning holes in the crown of my hat.

"That badge you carry worth shit?"

"Just about." I put away the notebook.

He fumbled then in a pocket on the side of the recliner and drew out a Ziploc bag containing brown cuttings and a handful of Zigzag papers and rolled himself the neatest joint you ever saw, licking the paper and without twisting the ends. "I axe you to join me but I got just enough to take me through the end of the month."

I cocked a palm and he put away the makings and came up with a wooden kitchen match and fired it off his square thumbnail the way no one knows how to do it anymore.

The cuttings caught quickly and the familiar stench thickened the air. He sucked in air and some smoke.

"That the goods, yours cut out on you too?" The dope constricted his vocal cords. He had sounded like a man gargling washers to begin with.

I said it was.

"Leave a note?"

I nodded.

He took another drag. Then he rolled over onto the gun and pulled a frayed brown leather wallet out of his left hip pocket. The joint burned between his fingers while he separated a limp shred of paper from the rest of the contents. He held it out and I got up to take it.

It was a half-sheet of ruled pulp torn from a tablet and folded in quarters. It had worn through at the creases and almost fell apart when I opened it. The message was written in smeared pencil in a round, childlike hand: "Joe, I sit here day after day watching you rub resin on that bow, stroking it like you used to do me and then putting it away without ever playing. I'm sick of it. I'm sick of you. Don't waste your time looking for me." It was unsigned.

"I did a lot of muggles that night," he said. "That was taped to the mirror in the crapper when I rolled out around noon. I left it up there six months and took it with me when I closed the place up. That and my bass, that's all I took. Everything else is still in there. I bought this place furnished and here I stay. What I get for marrying a girl was born the day I played the Astor."

I gave back the note. "Try to find her?"

"I had the cops in. Fat sergeant looked at the note and told me to wait for the divorce papers. I never got them. I waited a couple of months and swallowed a bottle of Bayers. Threw 'em right back up. If I had Fanny then I guess we wouldn't be talking." He showed me his gums again. "Joke is, I ain't been up to playing that big fiddle for ten years. I sit there holding it between my legs and I can't get from one note to the next. Them two sonsabitches couldn't of taken anything I got less use for. Maybe I should of told her."

"It wouldn't have changed anything. Nobody leaves because of a bad habit. It's just a screen." Standing over him I was starting to feel hollow-headed. Whoever his source was, he wasn't stopping at Acapulco. It was Bogotá or bust with him.

"Really the blues, man." He took in some smoke and held most of it and released the rest. "Hell of it is, I can't even use them."

I hung at the door. "Do you need anything?"

He looked up at me for a long time from under his mantel of forehead. He'd forgotten who I was.

"A great big juicy slice of nineteen fifty-five," he said. "That's what you can get me. I ate it too fast the first time."

I thanked him for the information and let myself out into the yard, into the cold sweet air of the yard.

4

My lungs could take only so much fresh air. I lit a Winston off the dash lighter, deadening the new-car stink a little, and started the engine. The house Sweet Joe Wooding didn't live in anymore didn't look so empty as I left the driveway. It was as full as a sick old man's skull and almost as dark.

I took Ford Road onto the Edsel Ford and followed it into Detroit. The sky was pewter and the air tasted of it, promising more snow. The city under it, flat rows of houses and two-story shops bristling into a fistful of skyscrapers as I continued east, had a grainy look, like the pictures of Stalingrad after the siege, or of Berlin cowering under clouds of Allied bombers. The river was choppy and smoke-colored. Windsor was a line of broken shadows on the other side. Some of the drivers had their lights on downtown, pale yellow circles in the dusklike Michigan winter morning.

When people come up missing you go to one end or the other to find them, never the middle. If you have a jumping-off point, a place where they were last seen or a person who had seen them last, you go there first, and I had done that. If that doesn't turn anything you go back to where they were first seen, but I couldn't afford the trip to Jamaica and Iris couldn't afford to send me. What Wooding had told me about George Favor saying he sat in sometimes at the Kitchen was a thin place to try and get your thumbnail under. If Favor was lying to save face it wasn't a place at all. But sometimes the lies are as good as the truth and anyway I had nothing else to scratch at but a thirty-year-old snapshot of a man who hadn't looked like himself in years.

The Kitchen was a corner establishment on one of the broken streets that wind through the warehouse district, one block up from the Renaissance Center, from where you could look down a double row of scorched brick buildings with discolored panes in their windows and heaps of blasted paving and see the Center's towers glistening at the end; the old Detroit with its hackles up snarling and lunging at the dainty heels of the new. Some of the warehouses had been converted into office buildings, not very convincingly, and the local press was starting to call the whole area Rivertown. The rats there are as big as condos.

I left the car with some others in a little gravel lot and let myself through a heavy oak door into a narrow entryway scabbed over with black-and-white pictures in glass frames. In them, bored-looking policemen in baggy uniforms stood on docks with their thumbs hooked in their belts watching men in fedoras and tight overcoats strapping crates onto the running boards of medieval-looking cars. The restaurant had been a speakeasy when the Purple Gang shot it out with the Coast Guard and their rivals the Licavolis on the river, and unlike the current administration it was proud of that part of Detroit's past. The original sliding peek-a-boo panel was still in the door and the oak-plank tables, carved all over with initials, had shelves underneath where drinks could be placed out of sight of passing policemen, as if they hadn't had enough incentive to look the other way in the first place. Newspaper headlines from Prohibition plastered the ceiling posts and there was a small platform in one corner for live entertainment in the evenings. The lights were dim and salmon-colored.

"One for lunch?" A pint-size hostess of eighteen or nineteen looked at me through orange bangs. She had a silver star pasted on her right cheek and a set of bracelets on both arms that clanked when she slid a laminated menu out of a wall rack. Black sacklike sweatshirt over ratty jeans and gold sandals. She went with the décor like tear gas.

"It's a little early," I said, although the place was already filling up. "Manager handy?"

"I'll say."

I grinned and she went to fetch him, carrying the menu. I watched her little round jean-covered rump going away. It made me feel like a child molester.

Presently she returned trailing a large heavy young man in a black processed suit and white shirt with a black knitted necktie. He had a head on me, which was going some, and outweighed me by sixty pounds, all of it babyfat. His light brown hair was plastered down like a seal's coat and he had pale blue eyes in a scrubbed pink face without a trace of whiskers. The other kids would have called him fatty, and not so long ago. His face wore a pink concerned look.

"Sir, is something the matter?"

I gave him a card. "I'm looking for a man named George Favor, a musician. He used to play here."

He looked annoyed. Expressions showed on big soft faces like his like thumbprints in lard. "Come back tonight and talk to Zelinka. Zelinka manages here nights and books all the talent."

"He might not have been booked. He told someone he sat in sometimes."

"Talk to Zelinka." He gave me back my card and went back the way he'd come. I looked down at the card. No one had ever done that before.

"Blubber-butt." The orange-haired hostess curled a lip at his back.

I put the card away. "Who's Zelinka, a belly dancer?"

"Drago Zelinka. We just call him Z. He like throws out the scumbags and puts back everything that fat jerk screws up during the day. Hog-bucket's only temporary while the real manager's in California. The rest of the time he stands here being fat and I wait tables."

"Isn't that a step up?"

A small nose got wrinkled. "Shit. Nobody tips the hostess."

I gave her a dollar. "Tell Z what I want to talk to him about, okay? A trombonist named George Favor. I'll be back tonight."

She put the bill in the pocket of her jeans and smiled at me. She had a gold tooth right in front.

Back at the office I picked up the mail and filed the bills in the wastebasket. There wasn't a final notice in the batch. That left me with a one-time-only chance to cruise the Caribbean and an advertisement for a correspondence course in forensic chemistry. I filed the advertisement with the bills and stapled the cruise brochure with its picture of a white ship on a cobalt sea to the corkboard on the wall next to the desk.

I called my service for messages. I burned some tobacco. I dusted the telephone and sharpened some pencils. A shaft of wood insisted on beating the lead to the point and I kept resharpening it until I had a razor tip and an inch and a half of pencil. I put it in the drawer and stood the others on their erasers in the chipped cup, arranging them into a bouquet. I dumped the shavings into the wastebasket. I was having a busy morning.

It didn't much matter if any customers came in or if I sat there all day weaving a bulletproof vest out of paperclips. The walls were soaked stud-deep in clients' problems and they were all beginning to sound depressingly alike. Mr. Detective, my husband is missing. Mr. Detective, my employees are stealing me blind. Mr. Detective, my wife is missing. Mr. Detective, my daughter is marrying a man next month and so far no one knows who he is or how many wives he's murdered. Mr. Detective, my son is missing. It was getting so I couldn't see them for the furniture. The same pinched women sitting with their knees together and their fingernails lined up on their purses in their laps, the same middle-aged men in pinstripes and reps and something screaming behind their tired faces, the same couples grown to resemble each other at a rate identical to the rate at which they had fallen out of love, not quite hating each other yet but getting there. They all stumbled down my hole with hope in their faces and despair in their eyes, animated ore cars forced off their worn wobbly rails by the reason I was in business. Even when I was able to give them what they asked for I was never sure if I had given them what they wanted. People aren't pencils.

They call it burnout. They have a name for everything and it never sounds like what it is. Burning and rotting aren't at all similar.

I got out the typewriter and updated my report for Axel Rainey. That started me thinking about Clara, and thinking about Clara reminded me of Astaire's steakhouse that used to be Harold's Hotcake Hacienda and I called there. A bright feminine voice thanked me for calling and asked me to call back after noon. It told me it was a recording. Even that made it happy.

Hanging up, I checked my watch. Ten minutes to twelve. I locked the door to the inner office and left the waiting room open and had lunch in the diner down the street, where the soup du jour tasted like yesterjour and the grilled cheese sandwich tasted like never again. When I got back Iris was in the waiting room.

She had on a leaf-yellow blouse tied at the waist over a burlap-colored tube top and a long green skirt that when she rose from the upholstered bench turned out not to be a skirt at all, but loose flared slacks. Culottes, they're called. Toeless shoes with cork soles. She wasn't wearing the turban. Her hair was longer now, waving at the collar and pushed over on one side. She used to wear it cropped very close. The new style softened the Egyptian effect.

I said, "You must be freezing."

"I came downtown to buy something warmer," she said. "I've never been to your office before. It's kind of like you."

"Old and cheap?"

"You're not old."

I dredged up a grin. "Wait till you see the rest."

I unlocked the inner door and held it for her without getting my arm in the way. I never could identify the scent she wore. Maybe it was just her. She looked around while I was climbing out of the outdoor gear. She'd left hers, a tan woolen coat and a yellow beret, on the bench outside. "Looks honest."

"I didn't think it was that bad." I pulled out the customer chair for her. I had unbolted it from the floor finally. Salesmen's breath didn't bother me nearly as much as it used to. Neither did salesmen. They didn't have any problems to unload, just merchandise. We sat down.

"I feel like I'm being interviewed for a job," she said.

"I'd use the sofa but you might suspect my intentions."

"Have you found out anything?"

"Nothing to report. I'm pretty much where you were last night."

"Do you have to?"

I had opened a fresh pack of cigarettes. I put it down without taking one. "I didn't know you quit."

"I gave them up on the island. Couldn't get my brand, and anything's easy after you kick dope."

"I never thought you would. Not for good."

"Well, we won't know I have until I don't."

"Small talk." I pointed at her purse, green satin with a bronze clasp, trapped between her hip and the arm of her chair. "Is that as well armed as the last one?"

"Yes."

"It's got something to do with why you're here and I'm not smoking?"

"I'm here to buy a pair of boots. And to find out how you were coming along."

I sat back. If they won't bite you can't make them. "You were right about Wooding," I said. "He's sick and scared. But he gave me some line and I'll run it out as soon as you leave."

"Oh." She made no move to get up.

"Who's after you?"

"One of my old customers."

"Which one and for what?"

"I don't know."

I said uh-huh. I wanted a smoke.

"I checked into a motel my first two days in town. I didn't want to show up at Mary M's unannounced with two suitcases. Third morning, the day I moved out, I found this in my jewelry box."

She handed me a three-by-five index card. Someone had drawn a crude skull-and-crossbones on the blank side in red ink, a keyhole shape with two circles for eyes and an X underneath. The ruled side was blank. It was dog-eared and a little dirty. I laid it on the blotter next to my cigarettes. "What makes it a customer?"

"The box has a false bottom. It's where I used to put the johns' money. Some of them probably saw me do it, in fact I'm sure some of them did. You don't think like a normal human being with that juice in your veins. That's where the card was, right in the middle under the false bottom."

"Jewelry boxes without false bottoms are rare. Anyone could figure it out. Or it could have worked its way out of a crack or something after a long time and you just never spotted it before. It doesn't look new."

"I looked in the box the night before. It wasn't in there then."

"Leave the room?"

She nodded. "That was my first night at Astaire's."

"Talk to the motel dick?"

"The night manager, whatever they call them now. He thought it was a joke and I couldn't prove anyone had been in the room after I left. I had a cheesy lock on the ground floor at the back. Place had entrances on every corner."

"Could just be someone playing pirate."

"What I thought, until somebody put a bullet through my windshield."

"I'm going to light up now," I said.

She nodded again and I did it and blew smoke away from her.

"I wasn't in the car," she said. "I parked on the street in front of Mary M's and when I came out for the suitcases I saw the hole, about head-high on the driver's side. Bullet's somewhere in the seat, I guess. I couldn't have been inside five minutes."

"No one saw or heard anything?"

"Nobody inside. I didn't canvass the neighborhood."

"Care to guess who put it there?"

She shook her head. "I tended to satisfy my customers."

"Who knows you're in town?"

"Just Mary M, and she didn't know until I called her after I found the card. I always use phony names in motels; old habit. Alice Irving, if it means anything."

"Whoever loaned you the car knows."

"Not really. It belongs to my fiancé's old partner in the fishing business. He's in overseas tours now and he keeps the car in a garage downtown for emergencies and for his friends to use. Charles gave me the claim slip. That's my fiancé. I never saw anyone, just the attendant at the garage."

"What's the friend's name?"

She thought. "I forget. Is it important?"

"I won't know that until he tells me. Can you call Charles and ask him?"

"I'd rather not. I haven't told him anything about this. He didn't want me to come here to begin with."

I got the location of the garage from her. While I was at it I got the name of the motel she'd stayed in and wrote it all down. "Make a list," I said. "Even Gandhi had enemies. And get out of Mary M's."

"You don't know her. I'm as safe there as anywhere."

"Just like your car."

"I mean inside."

"Why didn't I hear about this last night?"

She put her purse in her lap. "Looking for my father for free is enough. Anything more would have to be interpreted as taking advantage. Somewhere there has to be a trade."

"Engaged goods are outside my reach."

She started to get up.

"Sit," I said. "It shouldn't come as any surprise to you how big a jackass I can be."

"Remembering it and seeing it are different." She remained standing. "I only came to ask if you'd dug up anything. The other thing just came out. Stick with Georgie Favor, please. It took a long time but I'm all grown up now."

"The bigger you get the more you need. No charge for the cracker-barrel philosophy."

"I'm glad."

"Did you drive the car here?"

"It's in the lot down the street."

I stood. "Let's go down and look at the bullet."

5

It was a butterscotch-colored Malibu, two years old, with a few parking dings in the doors but otherwise unmarked except for a clean hole in the windshield about where the eyes focused driving. The tip of my little finger just fitted it. A rip in the back of the driver's seat where foam rubber was poking out through the tan vinyl said the gun had been fired at about a thirty-degree angle downward. The glass around the hole looked scorched. I leaned over and sniffed at it, jerking my head back involuntarily the way you do when sulfur puckers your nostrils.

I looked around. Iris and I were alone at that end of the lot. The black attendant at the entrance was busy adjusting dials on the radio in his booth. Unclipping the Smith & Wesson from my belt inside my coat, I placed the muzzle against the hole. I had to do it with my left hand in order to duplicate the angle. That tied it to someone who was either right- or left-handed, or maybe he was ambidextrous; anyone can fire a shot with his off hand if accuracy doesn't count. I holstered the gun and opened the door and got out my pocket knife. After ten minutes and as many curses my fingers closed around a hard lump inside the seat and I pulled out a conical piece of lead the size of a fat eraser. The tip was flattened slightly.

"What will that tell anyone?" Iris asked.

"Nothing, if our boy didn't shoot someone with the same gun fairly recently." I straightened, brushing pills of yellow foam rubber off my coat, wrapped the bullet in my handkerchief, and put it in my coat pocket. "If he did, ballistics will have it on file at thirteen hundred."

"Police." She said it the way you might expect her to, given her background.

"As a rule I don't get any better treatment from them than you did when you were working," I said. "Worse, probably. But I've got a pipeline of a sort. He doesn't have to know where the bullet came from."

"I like that part."

I slammed the door. The attendant in the booth swung his head in our direction, then turned up the volume on his radio. The Temptations rattled the glass in the windows. I said, "Your admirer is still on a warning binge. He doesn't want to hurt you yet or he wouldn't be leaving notes and shooting into empty cars. He's got to come out of the wings sometime to tell you what he wants, or doesn't want. If we do this right we'll know who he is before he gets around to it."

"We?"

"Me looking, you staying put. Don't go out unless you can't avoid it, and then take somebody you trust with you. And make that list."

"You mean like nuts with guns? I had some of those."

"I'm not surprised. This town's full of them. Some of them are judges. I mean like anybody dark or hostile or who acted like his brains boiled too long, or not long enough. You know the formula."

"That doesn't leave many," she said. "It wouldn't help. Nobody ever gives his right name."

33

"See what you can come up with anyway."

"Do I rate a bodyguard?"

"Do you want one?"

She shook her head. The yellow beret was bright against the gray granite around us. "I'm sleeping solo these days."

"Bodyguards are just nightlights, like fingerprinting your kids at school. It means their corpses can be identified."

"Also gives Big Brother a line on them early."

"That's ACLU's headache. I'll drive you home. We can pick up your car later."

She patted my cheek and opened the door and slid in under the wheel. "Find my old man." The engine ground over twice and caught.

I leaned an arm on the open door. "Any chance somebody doesn't want him found?"

"They had to have followed me all the way from Kingston. I was just starting to ask questions here when that card turned up in my jewelry box. Why would somebody not want him found?"

"I don't know. Probably the two things have nothing to do with each other. Life doesn't hang together that neat. I'm just spitballing."

She put the car in gear but left her foot on the brake. I stepped back. Grasping the door handle she looked up at me with thought on her face. "Are you getting enough sleep? You look beat."

"The kind of beat I am sleep can't cure," I said. "Call me if it rains."

She said she would and pulled the door shut and backed out of the space. After she hit Grand River I stood on the corner and smoked a cigarette. None of the cars parked against the curb pulled out behind her. A rattletrap Pinto hatchback with a busted tailpipe left the lot a couple of minutes later but turned in the other direction with an old lady at the wheel. I went back to the office.

———

I called police headquarters and while it was ringing I took the bullet out of my pocket and looked at it. A property clerk answered, went away, and came back to tell me Lieutenant John Alderdyce was on indefinite leave.

"Since when?"

"Since last week," the clerk said. "Is it an emergency?"

I hung up and tried John's home number. The line was busy. It was still busy a minute later and I called Astaire's.

The bright voice answered again, but this time it was live. I asked if Darryl Astaire was back from his trip. She put me on hold.

He came on a moment later, a deep quiet voice like wrapped thunder. He was cautious at first when I told him who was calling, but when he found out it wasn't about Clara Rainey he loosened up a notch. He didn't know anyone named George Favor. When he bought Harold's he'd let the kitchen staff go and replaced the dishwasher with a machine. If he kept up with the lives of all the people he'd had to fire, he said, he wouldn't have time to look after his present employees.

"Would Harold know?"

"I doubt it. He moved to Texas, where I heard he died."

I drew an empty circle on my telephone pad, a face without features. I had run out of questions. "Okay. Thanks, Mr. Astaire."

"Thank *you*. For holding off telling Clara's husband."

"How is she?"

"She took the day off. She should be with him now."

"Good luck."

"It's been nothing but good since she came here." He thanked me again and hung up.

John's line was still busy. The name of the motel Iris had stayed in her first three days in town stared up at me from the pad, next to the blank face. I looked it up in the telephone directory, then decided to go there in person.

35

I still had my hat and coat on and it would be a shame to waste them. I took along the bullet.

It was steel cold in the car. The wheel was icy and when I hit the ignition cold air stiffened my face and went down my collar before I got the heater fan switched off. It was getting dark out at just past one in the afternoon. I drove the entire twenty-odd blocks without seeing a scrap of color. When it's February in Detroit it's been winter forever.

The motel took up a block of Tireman, two square red-brick buildings connected by a walkway sealed in clear plastic with its name out front in green neon. In the parking lot a slim black youth in a red blazer walked from car to car recording license plate numbers on a sheet attached to a metal clipboard. I passed under a canopy into a generous lobby for an overnight place, paved in gray tile and containing a plastic reservation desk molded to resemble carved maple. There were no chairs or benches. Exotic-looking plants grew out of squat concrete planters, but they had thought of those too and set big spikes around the edges to discourage anyone from sitting on them. You can tell a lot about hotels and motels by their lobbies.

The towheaded clerk was speaking into a red telephone to match his blazer. He wore a black clip-on bow tie and an arsenal of ballpoint pens in a plastic holder in his handkerchief pocket. One of them was gone from the holder and he was using it to write something on a buff pad with the motel's name printed across the top. Up close he had a pale moustache whose hairs reminded me of the spikes in the planters. I propped an elbow on the desk and waited for him to finish his conversation. After five minutes he said good-bye and glanced at me and worked the plunger and pecked out a number and spoke to someone else. Ten minutes later he said good-bye again and punched some more buttons. I waited until he started talking, then stretched out an arm and pressed down the plunger.

He glared and got his mouth into gear. It was a feminine mouth, pink-lipped and mobile under the spiky growth. "What do you—" He closed it again when he saw the buzzer.

"Two calls when a customer's standing in front of you, okay. Three is abusing the privilege." I snapped shut the folder. "I want to see the house man."

He went through an open door at the back without saying anything. While he was gone I stood around scowling at my watch every couple of seconds and looking like I had an ulcer and troubles at home, just in case he was watching me through a crack. Real cops don't act like that, but he didn't look as if he'd been on the job long enough to know a real cop from his clip-on.

He came back in finally and picked up the telephone and slotted himself between me and it while he used the buttons. That wasn't necessary, because I'd lost interest in him. A very tall, bald, gray-eyed man in a well-cut gray suit had entered behind him, and this was a different number altogether. He had a gray silk tie on a gray shirt and a gray moustache that looked to be the grandfather of the bristle on the towhead's lip and when he spoke his voice was gray.

"I'm the night manager, Mr. Charm," he said. "And you are?"

"The name's a gag, right?"

The moustache twitched. "I assure you, no. Has there been a complaint? One of our guests?"

I returned his serve. "Lady claims her room was broken into night before last. She couldn't get any satisfaction from the help so she came to us."

He drew a slim notebook bound in gray leather from an inside pocket and started leafing through it. "Name?"

"Alice Irving."

"Oh yes." He shut it and returned it to his pocket. "Someone's idea of a joke."

"Breaking and entering is funny?"

"There was no sign of forced entry. She reported nothing missing. Guests are often mistaken about such things. They neglect to pack something and immediately assume it's been stolen."

"How many report something was added?"

The moustache twitched again. It was round and thick and groomed sleek as a greyhound. "May I see your badge, Mr. . . . ?"

"Walker." I flashed it, not quick enough. I saw it in the gray eyes.

"I have one of those too," he said. "The sheriff's department used to auction them off whenever they changed designs until too many private licenses started showing them around. Are you aware of the penalty for impersonating a police officer, Mr. Walker?"

"They vary according to the judge. And I never said I was an officer."

"Just having the badge could get your license suspended. At the very least. I could have you escorted from the premises, but you saw the door on your way in."

"I saw your security too. Forget it." I pocketed the folder. "We're in the same racket, Mr. Charm. I'm just trying to find out who ran up the Jolly Roger in Miss Irving's room. The motel doesn't have to come into it."

He ran a thumb down his necktie, lining it up with the placket of his shirt. "If you'd come to me straight on instead of trying to intimidate me with authority I might have cooperated, inasmuch as I can cooperate in a matter that has nothing to do with this establishment. Now you can just take your tin shield out the door."

"Don't get your feathers up," I said. "Hotel dicks are old

scenery to me. A lot of them run with the roosters. If you don't, that's okay. But don't get all fogged up because I didn't expect you not to."

It smoothed him a little. He did the thing with the tie again.

"We're not unreasonable," he said. "The comfort and safety of our guests come first. It's just that I'm not convinced that Miss Irving wasn't mistaken. That card could have been placed among her things by a friend before she came here, as a joke."

"She's not laughing."

"I didn't say it was a good joke. The nature of her personal relationships is not our concern."

"That's how it is."

"I'm afraid so."

The clerk was sneering at me with the red telephone screwed to his ear. I took my elbow off the desk.

"One more question. What's the night manager doing on duty in the daytime?"

Charm smiled thinly without disturbing the moustache. "The title is a euphemism. Like 'private investigator' for cut-rate gumshoe."

"I was right," I said. "The name's a gag."

I took myself out of the lobby. The black youth with the clipboard had worked his way down to the far end of the parking lot and was starting back my way. I intercepted him. He had his hair moussed up into a tall flattop the way they wear it now and a crescent of dark beard on the end of his long chin. His only concession to the cold was a thin green-and-white-striped scarf flung around his neck. The company blazer looked as thick as a handkerchief. He looked me over with great brown eyes and waited. Our breath made jets in the air.

"How much they pay you to take down license plates?" I asked.

"Who's interested?"

"The Lincoln twins." I held up two five-dollar bills.

"That's two and a half hours," he said. "Not that it ever takes me ten minutes. I write them all down and then I come around again a hour later, see how many's parking here ain't registered. They still here in another hour they gets towed."

"Were you on duty night before last?"

He glanced at the bills and I gave them to him. He hiked the clipboard under his arm and folded them over, smoothing the crease between long brown fingers. "Six to ten. They rotates me."

"I need a list of the numbers that didn't belong that were parked here that night. They don't have to have showed up more than once. The one I want probably didn't. He'd have parked out back, then again maybe not."

"Mr. Charm gots all the lists in his office."

"I bet he doesn't lock the door every time he leaves it."

"How much you bet?"

I pointed at the bills. "Two more brothers. If there's a list."

"There's one." He bent his head around to read my watch. "He goes off at three to rest up for night duty."

I gave him the card the acting manager at the Kitchen had returned to me. "Leave a message with my service if I'm not there." I watched him tuck the card inside the fold of the bills and put them in the side pocket of his blazer. "I'd as soon throw those down a storm drain as not get a call."

"You get it. Lester Hamilton ain't Mr. Charm." He carried the clipboard inside.

6

I filled up at a station on Tireman and tried John Alderdyce's home number again from the pay telephone.
The line was still tied up. I got in and drove.

His house was one of a dozen in a cul-de-sac off Fenkell,
beige tile over concrete block with the standard garage
extension on the end with the usual basketball hoop mounted
over the open door and the obligatory bicycles and garden
tools and pop bottles wedged in on both sides of a Japanese
car. I could hear the television pulsing inside when I used
the bell. After a long time the door opened and the man
stood there in an unbuttoned brown cardigan and jeans
and stocking feet with a bottle of Miller in one hand. He
was thick through the chest and shoulders and big in the
head with a shelf of bone over his eyes and a jaw you could
build a small house on. His skin was black with a purplish
tint, and looking at him you knew he would always be the
bad cop in the interrogation room. Behind him the television was still droning.

"Walker."

He had always called me that, going back to when we
were kids; never Amos. I said, "They told me at thirteen

41

hundred you were on personal time. Who's on the telephone?"

"I took the fucking thing off the hook. The department shrink can't stop playing with that dial and every time he plays with it he uses my number. Take it in out of the cold."

The house was warm. He hung my hat and coat on the hall tree and offered me a beer. I said no thanks and he tipped his up, emptying it, and set it down at the end of a row of empties on the kitchen counter and opened the refrigerator and twisted the top off a fresh one. I followed him into the carpeted living room, where on the 21-inch screen a pile of gray hair in a suit with wide lapels was working his way with a microphone through an audience of women, asking them what they thought of lesbian postal clerks.

"Fucking faggot." John turned off the set and flung himself into a scoop chair upholstered in green vinyl. I sat on the edge of a green plaid sofa in the only spot that wasn't piled with magazines and record albums. The floor was a litter of crumpled socks and sports sections and stray lint. The butt of another empty stuck out from under John's chair.

"So what's doing in rental heat these days?" he asked.

"Same old same old. A keyhole here, a kidnaped heiress there. The rest of the time I'm shaking blondes and hand grenades out of my bed. Where's Marian?"

"Visiting her parents in Flint. She took the kids with her."

"I guess you couldn't get away."

"Her old man's in construction. City employees are people he pays to tie their shoelaces while his people dump sand into the cement. We get on like salt and iron. Her mother plays bingo."

"You've been alone here how long?"

"Let's see, I had ten cases when I started. A week."

I didn't see his department piece anywhere. The only weapon visible, not counting the alcohol, was a deer rifle with mounted scope leaning in one corner. "You under hack downtown?"

"No." He tilted the bottle and set it down. Foam climbed to the neck, then collapsed. "I'm sick to puking of paperwork up the wazoo and cops who are starting to look and sound like the mayor and TV pricks asking why did you chase that boy who raped and strangled the little old lady and stole her car, put all those other motorists in jeopardy? I'm sick of civil liability and toy coffee in the office pot. I want caffeine. We've got more contract killers in uniform than we've got in the mugs and I'm sick of that. I'm on vacation."

"For how long?"

He lifted the bottle again and studied the contents, three quarters gone. "I've got six cases left on the back porch. When I've killed them I'll decide."

"That'll be Friday at the rate you're going."

He looked at me, eye-whites glittering in his dark brutal face. "Run your errand or give me a pamphlet and go. I want a lecture I'll put the phone back on the hook."

I thought of leaving. My welcome with friends wasn't going too far lately. I stayed where I was. I took out my handkerchief and unwrapped the bullet and held it out.

He made no move to take it. "Dig it out of anyone I know?"

"Out of a seat in a lady's car. You wouldn't remember her. She was stuck on the edge of the Freeman Shanks case a few years back. I want to put it to a gun. Who do I see while you're on vacation?"

"Talk to Hornet."

"Next suggestion."

He belched. "Try Lieutenant Thaler in Robbery. Use

43

my name. Thaler's got priority in ballistics in cases not related to homicide. City hall wants to bring down those statistics before the Grand Prix in June."

I rewrapped and pocketed the bullet. While I was doing that he finished his beer and went into the kitchen and came back with another. He'd left the empty on the coffee table and now he rearranged some newspapers to make room for it, uncovering the black rubber butt of his revolver in its burgundy leather holster. Just for fun I asked him if he'd ever heard of a jazz trombonist named George Favor.

"Little Georgie."

I'd been looking at the scribbles in my notebook. Now I raised my eyes. His face was a little less grim, like Rushmore in misty light.

"Dad took me to one of his concerts in the old Walled Lake Pavilion. I was nine or ten. I guess there were better on the trombone, but I didn't know it. Neither did he. Give me a second."

He got up, found his balance, and came over to the sofa. He spent a couple of minutes shuffling through the records piled there, then muttered something and left the room. I helped myself to a slug of his beer while he was gone. I had never seen him swaying before. The house smelled stale. I lit a cigarette.

He came back carrying a thick record in a stiff green paper sleeve and lifted the lid on the console stereo. "Could have bought a new one for what it cost me to have this thing fixed," he said, adjusting the controls. "You can't get 78 rpm anymore."

The needle swished and crackled for half a minute, like surf breaking. There was a short guitar lick followed by a piano and then a sweet low sound sliding up and down and all around "Old Rocking Chair" without ever actually touching the melody. It was there, yet not, like the vermouth in a skillfully made martini; a cool cloud drifting. Favor hadn't the warmth of a Tommy Dorsey or the casual genius of a Jack Teagarden. He wouldn't have held the public ear long and his talent wouldn't have earned him underground legend as a musician's musician. But he was too good to wind up washing dishes in a flapjack joint. I listened to it all the way through, John standing next to the console out of the way of the speakers, and laid a column of ash into an empty tray on the coffee table that hadn't been used in a while. It meant something that John hadn't taken up smoking again after quitting eleven times.

"I'm surprised I never heard of him," I said.

"No reason you would have. He didn't have the stuff to break the color line when it would have counted. What makes him important now?"

"Woman I'm working for just found out she's Favor's daughter." I told him the rest of it, leaving out the threats against Iris. I didn't know where they plugged into it myself, or if they did.

The stereo arm had swung back and switched itself off. He turned the record over. "This the same woman belongs to the bullet?"

"Yeah."

"Why don't these people go to the cops." It was rhetorical. He turned the stereo back on and picked up his beer. "Try the union?"

"After I run down this Kitchen lead."

Following the opening lick on the second side a woman's voice came in, clear as grain alcohol:

> *I'm yesterday's lady, tomorrow you'll be too.*
> *I'm yesterday's lady, tomorrow you'll be too.*
> *Today this lady's leaving, lose these yesterday blues.*

"Who's the singer?"

"A man's name. Glen something. It's on the label."

45

The chorus was repeated and then the band came back on, Favor's horn laying down background. When the side finished, John took the record off the turntable and held it out.

" 'Vocal by Glen Dexter,' " I read. "What happened to her, I wonder?"

"Went to dope and died happily ever after, probably." He put it back in its sleeve and laid it atop the console. "What's Joe Wooding like?"

"Old and scared and alone. His wife left him and he shut up her ghost in the house and moved into a trailer out back. He's dying."

"I thought he was dead already. It makes you feel cheated."

"You're starting to remind me of him."

That shook him to his toes. He changed hands on the bottle.

"What happened?" I said.

"She says I never talk. What am I supposed to do, come home and say, 'You'll never guess who I found carved into four manageable pieces and individually wrapped in Hefty bags today'? Wives, they watch some bitch with a Ph.D. on television and think talking fixes everything. Last summer we body-bagged two husbands, a wife, and a family of three because they started talking. Must be nice to have a place like Flint to run to."

I said nothing. He drank.

"I knew this prowl-car officer, Krebbs. Fat slob, his uniforms never fit him. Chief suspended him under consideration for dismissal after he weighed in at fifteen pounds over the limit, but he took his thirty years to the DPOA and got himself reinstated. He went through two wives in six years and there was talk he was shaking down some merchants on his patrol for protection. Everybody hated the bastard.

"Last month he was making an undercover arrest with

some suits in a safe house on Fort Street when a rookie from the First Precinct battered his way in and opened fire, thought it was a heist. Fucking little hot dog firing birdshot out of a forty-four mag. Krebbs blew his head off, but not before the little fucker put two good detectives on permanent disability. Department held a hearing and dropped Krebbs from roll call like a hot rivet. They wanted to bring charges against him for manslaughter, only somebody in IAD had placed him under felony advisement and you can't do both under the Constitution."

"I read about it."

"Week or so later Krebbs got drunk and ran his car into an abutment on the Jeffries. State cops said there was no sign he'd made any attempt to stop. A brother or somebody buried him in Wyandotte. No uniforms, no mayor or chief or inspectors at the funeral. He wasn't a cop anymore, see. The little hot dog with the magnum got the works.

"We used to stand tight," he said after a moment. "We used to stand tight."

He took one last swig and stood holding the bottle, bouncing it a little in his hand as if getting ready to throw it. Finally he stood it on the coffee table next to the other empty. "Kind of get the hell out of here, okay? Today even a private badge is more than I can take."

I got up. "Go skiing," I said. "Build a snowman. Cut a hole in the ice on Lake Erie and drop a line in and sit down and wait. The inside of one of those bottles looks pretty much like all the rest."

"I'll go out in a little while."

"Put the telephone back on the hook first."

After a space he smiled. It tightened the flesh over his big facial bones. "It'll drive the shrink crazy," he said. "He'll think I ate my revolver."

I grinned back. "When's this Lieutenant Thaler come on?"

"Six."

"Will we get along?"

He was still smiling. "You'll want to."

I stopped in the office to polish off my report on Clara Rainey and made out an invoice and dropped them into a manila envelope for mailing. When that was done I unhooked the paging device that looked like an oversize fountain pen from my breast pocket and tested it. It squawked healthily. I called my service to ask if anyone had left a message. No one had. I decided to give Lester Hamilton some more time to go through those license plates and went to the Kitchen for supper. It was nearly dark out at five o'clock and loose grains of snow were beginning to swarm in my headlamp beams. I scrubbed frost off the inside of the windshield with the heel of my hand.

The little gravel parking lot was full. I found a spot on the street and went inside, brushing snow off my shoulders, and let a young man I'd never seen before in a gold Eisenhower jacket escort me to a corner table cut off from the rest of the room by a thick oaken post. It was one of a very few tables not already occupied that early on a weeknight. The place at night was noisy with voices and the ceiling was becoming mythical with a blue cigarette haze forming between the rafters. Somebody I couldn't see fumbled with the microphone on the bandstand; an ear-splitting howl of feedback deadened the voices momentarily. I was about to ask the host to fetch Mr. Zelinka when music from Little Georgie Favor's trombone introduced itself into the room like a cold cloud drifting.

7

I didn't knock down the kid in the gold jacket or even push him out of the way. I went around him and stood in front of the bandstand, where a narrow white party in his late twenties was playing a silver trombone away from the microphone, circling his way around "Twelfth Street Rag" about two measures behind the usual tempo. He had lots of wavy brown hair to his shoulders that looked as if he combed it with his fingers and a beard that started just below his eyes and grew down his neck into his collar. The collar belonged to a blue knit pullover shirt under a rumpled white cotton jacket with the sleeves pushed up past his forearms. The rest was black chinos and prairie boots scuffed at the toes.

Behind him on the platform sat a soft fat young black man with white-framed glasses and a modest Afro, not playing a bass viol between his knees, and, behind a set of drums, another white man about the trombonist's age who I thought at first was an albino. At a second glance he had bleached his straight short hair the color of water. He had his sticks in one hand but he wasn't playing either, smoking a cigarette and reaching up from time to time to flick ash off the end without removing it from his lips. He had on a tight black vest over a ruffled pink shirt. The bass had breasts like a woman's under a white T-shirt and rings of fat around his middle.

When the trombonist finished his lick he lowered the instrument and another man joined him on the bandstand, bounding up and seizing the microphone. He was short and solid in a tailored midnight-blue suit and a cinnamon necktie laid beautifully on a white shirt with a soft collar. His beard was gunmetal under his smooth dark face and his black hair shone like bent painted steel in the overhead spot. He looked like a Drago Zelinka.

"Ladies and gentlemen, the Kitchen is proud to present the ice-cool jazz of L. C. Candy and Domino."

That bought a round of applause, and the smooth number stepped off as the trio slid into "Lullaby of Birdland," the drummer barely brushing the cymbals while the bass grunted and the trombone carried the melody. It sounded even more like Favor's when you were standing in front of it.

"Mr. Zelinka?"

The smooth number paused on his way past and turned slate-colored eyes on me. He was older than he looked under the platform spot, about fifty; there were lines around his eyes and the flesh under his chin was starting to sag. I had eight inches on him, but he had spent a lifetime looking at men who were taller than he was and could do it without seeming to raise his chin. A muscle moved in his face when I introduced myself. "My office is in back."

If he did any work there it didn't show. The desk was polished white maple with an ivory leather top, a pearl telephone and nothing else on it. The walls were paneled in darker maple and soundproof quilting covered the door. It thumped shut on the music, cutting it off like the lid of a music box. I pinched out my cigarette and dropped it into a square woodgrain wastebasket mounted on wheels. It was empty otherwise. The room had no windows.

He circled behind a tufted leather armchair, ivory to match the desktop, and rested his hands on the back. "You wanted to talk about George Favor."

"That's his music outside," I said. I stood in the middle of the neutral carpet with my hands in my pockets. His chair was the only one in the room. "Does Candy know him?"

"Just his music. He has every record Favor ever cut and he can play them all note for note, even the mistakes. The best make them, you know. The difference is after they make them they aren't mistakes anymore. When Candy auditioned by playing three of Favor's old standards I hired him on the spot."

He spoke careful English without an accent. I guessed Hungarian, but only from his name. "Sweet Joe Wooding says Favor told him he sat in here sometimes."

"I thought Wooding was dead."

"A lot of people are going to be surprised when they read his obituary in a month or so. Did Favor sit in here?"

"You haven't yet told me why you're looking for him."

I told him. After a moment he moved from in back of the chair but left one hand on it. He had large hands for a small man. One of them would have been enough to cover his face. "A few times, very late. Most of the customers who were still here at that hour could not have cared less, and I don't suppose he did either. He just wanted to play. The musicians were glad enough to have him."

"Candy wasn't one of them?"

"He's only been here a few months. He became excited when I mentioned Favor used to come in here and play. He asked me all kinds of questions about him, most of which I couldn't answer. He's a true fanatic."

"When did Favor stop coming in?"

The midnight-blue suit moved becomingly with his shoulders. "The nights blur together. How long does it take to notice that someone has stopped coming around? Two years ago, three. He couldn't have been doing it more than six months, and only eight or ten times then. It wasn't as if he were a regular."

"When Wooding saw him four years ago he told him he was playing here."

"It could be three. The nights all blur together as I said."

"You never heard where he went?"

"I assumed he died. He didn't look healthy at all and his wind wasn't too good. One solo to a set was as much as he could manage, and he had to sit down and wheeze between them." He paused. "I wasn't all that unhappy when he stopped coming in."

"I guess a dead man on the bandstand doesn't do much for business."

"It wasn't that. The musicians' union looks very darkly upon performers playing anywhere for free. I could have been picketed."

"Favor might not have been a member."

"That would have been even worse."

I took my hands out of my pockets. "Thanks for your time, Mr. Zelinka. Would it be all right if I spoke to Candy?"

"I don't know what good it would do. I said he wasn't here then."

"You also said he worships Favor. I can use anything worth knowing about the man I'm looking for, including his taste in ice cream. Who would know but a fan?"

"Fudge ripple. Or at least it was in the fifties. I don't know what it would be now. *Downbeat* hasn't written about him in thirty years."

We were sitting at my table by the ceiling post. The band was between sets, and Domino — the black bass man and the artificial albino—had left the platform, probably to share a wrinkled brown cigarette in the alley. Unlike Zelinka, L. C. Candy looked even younger away from the spot, about twenty-five, and he had the fresh shallow voice of a teenaged boy. A glass of Pepsi Free stood on his side of the table with ice in it and nothing else. He didn't smoke and I'd have bet my next car payment he never took dope. The new generation of musicians took some getting used to. I said, "How is it you know what *Downbeat* wrote about him thirty years ago? Your father would have been in high school."

"I got every issue that ever mentioned him, also Louis and Bird and Roy Eldridge. His records too, all fifteen of 'em." He sipped his Pepsi and crunched some ice. He had bright eyes that got brighter when he talked about Favor.

"You must've started early."

"Two years ago March. That's when I heard one of his records for the first time on the University of Michigan station. Dark ages for me, man. I was playing backup for the Pelicans in Ann Arbor."

"Never heard of them, sorry."

"You didn't miss anything. At the end of each concert we set fire to our instruments."

"You put out your trombone in time."

"I was playing guitar then. I went back to the 'bone after I heard Little Georgie. Rock's all gone to shit, but jazz—well, it's forever, man, you know what I'm saying?"

"You're not on the bandstand now," I said.

"Yeah. Shit. They expect us to talk like that. I've got an M.A. in Performing Arts and they want me to sound like I flunked gym." He picked up the straw he had taken out of his glass and bent it. "So you're working for Little Georgie's daughter? What's she like?"

"She's the best. You didn't know Favor used to play here before you auditioned?"

"It's not really such a coincidence. There aren't that many jazz places left in Detroit. The town's like that, always following the trend that's just past. When R-and-B was big it went Motown, and now that jazz is back it wants punk. Disco, don't even talk to me about disco. I got another set to do without throwing up."

"I didn't know jazz was back."

"Maybe it isn't. Maybe I'm just hoping. Too many limeys screwed up rock, took it away from us and took the roll out of it and after that we had to get high to enjoy it. Jazz is."

I hooked a beer from a waitress and asked if he wanted a refill. He shook his head. "Know anything about a girl singer named Glen Dexter?" I asked.

He perked. "Hell, yes. She could've been as big as Dinah Washington or Sarah. She retired early."

"She recorded with Favor once."

"Once, hell. She never cut with anyone else. They almost married."

"What happened?"

He shrugged. "It was a bad time for a white woman to hook up with a black man. Maybe that was it. They broke up is all I know. She sang at the Paradise Lounge afterward. Died sometime late in the sixties. I met her niece last year at the Montreux festival."

"Know where I can find her?"

"Ypsilanti, I think. She introduced herself because she said I sounded like Georgie. You can bet I pumped her about him. Edwina Dexter, that's her name." He pronounced it with a long *i*.

I wrote it down. "Either of your boys here when he used to sit in?"

"I was here first. Hey, you find him, call me, okay? I got a ton of questions to ask." He gave me a card.

It was printed on tangerine stock with his name and

address and telephone number in raised characters and a musical clef in one corner. I ran a thumb over the embossing. "What do the initials stand for?"

"Laverne Carroll."

"Thanks, L. C." I shook his hand. It was thickly calloused where the slide rested against his thumb and forefinger.

He returned to the platform for the next set and I ate something that sounded Italian and washed it down with beer and drove down to 1300 Beaubien, Detroit Police Headquarters. The snow was cuff-deep now and gave off its own light under the street lamps.

The squad room was quiet after the shift change, papered over with FBI circulars and typewritten memos and giving off an institutional smell of disinfectant and instant coffee and galoshes and the cat litter they threw on the floor where suspects lost their lunches. I asked for Lieutenant Thaler and a sad-faced plainclothesman in an underarm holster with egg salad on his tie jerked his thumb at an office door standing open. I went to it and rapped on the frame.

It was a square cubicle like all the rest, sequestered inside amber pebbled glass that fell a foot short of the squad room ceiling, but tidier than most. The paperwork was arranged in neat piles on the gray steel desk and bound copies of the Michigan Penal Code stood in order of year in a metal bookcase with a coffee machine on top, its little red light glowing. A spray of bright flowers grew out of a cut-glass vase on the corner of the desk opposite the telephone. Peonies, if it matters.

A trim woman in her mid-thirties sitting behind the desk looked up from her writing when I knocked. She had light brown hair that could have been honey blonde with no trouble, curling under at her shoulders and pushed back to form bangs on her forehead by a red plastic hairband like little girls wear. It didn't look out of place on her. She wore tortoiseshell glasses with large round frames and a tailored khaki suit with a white jabot frothing at her throat. The nameplate on the desk read LT. MARY ANN THALER.

She said, "Yes?" She had a dimple at the corner of her mouth and her forehead wrinkled a little when she raised her eyebrows.

"John Alderdyce said I'd want to get along with Thaler," I said after a moment.

She sat back and unscrewed her ballpoint pen. Her eyes flickered over me from behind the glasses. They were baby blue and nowhere near the size of hen's eggs. "You're not going to challenge me to an arm-wrestling match, are you?"

"Uh-uh. You might win. I've got a delicate ego."

"It looks like the only thing about you that is. You're with who?"

I opened my folder, turning the badge around back. It wasn't likely to impress her. "John's a friend. He said you had a leg up with ballistics."

"How is he?"

"Drinking Millers like Prohibition's coming back tomorrow. He'll be okay."

She screwed the pen back together, measuring me still. After a second she glanced at the chair in front of the desk. I sat down. She lifted the receiver off the telephone, dialed, waited a long time, spoke for a minute, and hung up. "John says you're okay."

"That's more than he ever said to me."

"He sounded drunk."

"That would explain it."

"What've you got for me?"

I unwrapped the bullet and laid it atop one of the piles of paper. She looked at it without picking it up.

"Thirty-eight. Where'd you get it?"

"Lady I'm working for found it in her driver's seat.

Someone put it through the windshield. She wasn't in the car at the time and she'd like to know who's responsible."

"Okay."

"Okay?"

She looked amused. "You want me to spell it?"

"I was expecting a lecture. Taxpayers' money and like that."

"I was one of four sergeants up for this promotion," she said. "The other three were black and one of them was a woman, and what do you think my chances were in the town that invented Affirmative Action? John took my jacket and my score on the looey's exam upstairs and didn't come back down until I had this spot. So when he says you're okay I figure you're up for Pope at least."

I scratched my ear.

"Something?"

"Just reconsidering my stand on women's rights."

"I was against them from the start. All those women running around fulfilling themselves while some poor schnook couldn't get a job to feed his family. Or hers." She unscrewed the pen. "Leave your card, Mr. Walker. I'll call if we raise anything."

8

The plow had just been down my street, followed by a salt truck to break up the ice the plow had uncovered and start dissolving my fenders and rocker panels. The cold air had frozen the ridges of snow hard as mortar and it was easier to pass a needle through the eye of a camel than to get into my driveway. I backed up and floored it and made it on the third try, tearing hell out of my new mud-guards and throwing brine as high as the windows. For-tunately, much of the car is plastic.

The house was chilly. There is something about trapping winter air that brings out the worst in it. I dialed up the thermostat and the oil furnace kicked in with the sound of a distant cash register. I plugged in the coffee maker and bought myself a drink from the cupboard bottle to start my blood moving. After a few minutes I took off my hat and coat to let the heat inside. The chill crept out of the place on slow club feet.

In my not-so-easy chair, sipping coffee laced with whis-key and listening to the click-clunk of the antique clock in the living room, I went over what I had. It wasn't much. It was less than that. So far I hadn't been able to establish an existence for Little Georgie Favor this side of three years ago. Where he went after the Kitchen was a question as wide as Detroit, or as narrow as an old man's options. I took out the picture Iris had given me of the two smiling people standing in front of the Piano Stool in Kingston. A happy young couple enjoying themselves for eternity, not knowing or caring what was coming, the moment lifted cleanly from time and set aside, like an item of token value rescued from an apartment before flames took it. Chief Crazy Horse was right. Cameras trapped the soul.

There were people I couldn't find. I had a drawerful of unfinished cases, most of them unpaid for too. Some of them just walked out on their lives and never went back. It's easier than you might think, and the more paper we have to carry around to prove we exist the easier it gets. In the last century you could run out to the territories, but communities were small and strangers stuck out a mile. Now it's just a question of getting hold of a birth certificate, which unlocks all the other paperwork, and getting swallowed up in a population center somewhere. Strangers are more common than acquaintances; no one thinks about them. They aren't even invisible. They're part of the scenery.

For all that, people who disappear according to plan are the most easily traceable. They trade in opposites. If they live in Los Angeles they move to New York City. If they're blond they dye their hair black. If they work in the accounting department they get a job hoisting crates of machine parts onto a loading dock. They take common names in place of unusual ones and nine out of ten of them wear their new lives like thorn underwear. You can pick them out of a crowd upside-down in a dirty mirror. The tough ones to find are the ones who left suddenly without thought, the thirty-year clerks who just missed being run over by stricken cab drivers on their way to work and the wives who walked into their husbands' offices and found them on the sofas with their secretaries — people who just turned away from their various crossroads and started walking with no idea of where they were heading. They took up lives similar to those they had left, sometimes in the next block and sometimes without even changing their names, and unless someone who knew them in their other lives ran into them in a supermarket you're out of luck. People don't pay private investigators to sit around waiting for coincidences. The success ratio isn't sparkling and even the most dedicated fishermen lose interest when their lines are slack as often as they're taut.

I didn't know which pigeonhole fitted George Favor. A man without friends glides around on the edge of others' vision. People never looked at him directly or noticed when he wasn't around until something happened to remind them. The job needed less work. Sometimes when you just let them lie, a root found its way into the soil and they blossomed on their own. The other job, the death's-head drawing in Iris' jewelry box and the bullet in her car, needed more work. The garage where she'd picked up the car was one handle. So far the attendant she'd claimed it from was the only person who knew she was in town. That was my all day tomorrow. When it comes to giving up information, garage attendants are as easy as doormen and confidential secretaries at the Pentagon. Clams were named for them.

I was still holding the picture. Having failed to draw any vibrations from it, I returned it to my breast pocket, brushing the paging device with my hand. I remembered Lester Hamilton then at the motel on Tireman, and as if that completed some sort of telepathic connection the beeper sounded. I turned it off and called my service. The girl said someone had left the name Lester and a number. I dialed it. He answered on the first ring.

"Mr. Walker?"

He sounded out of breath. I felt a tingling. He hadn't

called to tell me he'd turned up a license plate that didn't belong in the motel parking lot. I asked him anyway.

"Forget that," he said. "It's Mr. Charm. I'm in his office."

"Is he listening?"

"No."

The tingling was stronger now. "Can he be?"

He might have swallowed. You can't tell over the telephone. "No."

I told him to sit tight and got my hat and coat and started reeling in line.

9

The motel looked much the same at night. The parking lot was well lit and the sign splashed green neon on the snow at its feet. Lester was standing under the canopy when I swung into a slot near the entrance. He had on the same red blazer and green-and-white-striped scarf. He opened my door.

" 'S'go in the side," he said. His flattop was a little mussed but other than that he looked as calm as moonlight.

We went through a steel fire door around the corner from the main entrance, at the end of a corridor carpeted in orange sherbet that started at the unfriendly lobby. I didn't get close enough to tell if the blazer behind the desk contained the towheaded clerk with the spiky moustache who had sneered at me that afternoon. Long before we got to it we turned down a shorter corridor ending in a ridged glass door with PRIVATE stenciled in black on one of the horizontal ridges. Lester pushed it open and stood aside holding it against the pressure of the closer. I accepted the invitation.

It was a narrow room where work got done, unlike Drago Zelinka's office at the Kitchen. A paneled desk two steps inside the door held up a scribbled-over appointment calendar and a metal rack jammed with letters in envelopes and a telephone with one of those caddies that let you rest the receiver on your shoulder while you're going through the mail. There were a locked file cabinet and a gray steel safe and a clipboard attached to the wall by the desk with papers curling away from it. There was a window looking across the space between the two buildings at the windows of the rooms on that side. I turned up the Venetian blinds to determine that and closed them again. The walls were painted beige.

The carpet was shallow for easy cleaning and made of tough short black-and-brown fibers that wouldn't wear out quickly. Mr. Charm was lying on it in a fetal curl with his congested face to the door and one hand curved loosely around an imitation stag handle protruding two inches above the watch pocket of his gray vest on the left side. The vest was stained dark around it but aside from that he was as well turned out as ever, with the gray knot of his silk necktie snugged up under his Adam's apple and a soft shine on his black tasseled loafers and not too much cuff showing at his wrists. The round gray moustache was perfect. He'd approve.

"He didn't go off at three like usual." Lester had stepped inside, letting the door close. "His light was still on and the door was locked when I checked again at ten. No one had saw him. I slipped the lock."

His skin was as cold as it gets, which is colder than just about anything. Still squatting, I examined the knife handle without touching it. It looked like a standard Boy Scout jackknife, only larger. They sell them in army surplus stores from Fairbanks to Miami. I got up, looked at him, looked at the door. If the body hadn't been moved he could have got it while he was standing there holding the door open for his visitor. One thrust in and up by somebody who knew what he was doing. There were no heel marks on the carpet. The door had a button lock. It was just a matter of setting it on your way out.

Mr. Charm. He had twitched his moustache at me twice and called me a cut-rate gumshoe.

I went behind the desk. Light filtered down through frosted panels in the ceiling, but there was a gooseneck lamp on the desk as well, switched off. The bulb was cold. I switched it on, using my handkerchief now. His calendar was full to the end of the month, appointments inked in in a neat block hand like architects use. His last appointment for that day had been with the initials A. G. at noon, shortly before I'd met him. There were no cross-outs, no pages missing. No one had ever left this world more neatly. I asked Lester about A. G.

"That'd be Mr. Gordenier, the owner." He still sounded out of breath.

There were scratches around the lock of the safe. They could have been brand-new or years old. You just can't tell unless they've been exposed to the elements. I tugged at the handle. Locked.

"He's the only one had the combination," said Lester.

"Maybe he forgot it sometime. When did you see him last?"

"Just after you left. I give him today's license numbers. That's them there on the board."

The top sheet on the clipboard attached to the wall contained a double row of letters and numbers written in a slashing hand, with the day's date and 1 P.M. scrawled at the top. There were other lists for 11 A.M. and noon. I paged back further. There were two sets of three for each day. Both sets were seldom in the same hand; two sets, two shifts. At length I wrapped my hand and lifted the board off its hook. Setting it on the desk I pried up the clip and took them all out and shuffled through the cheap drug-store typing stock. A torn corner drifted out. I asked Lester if he had worked the night of February tenth.

He stroked his crescent of dark beard. "Night before last, yeah. Pulled two shifts."

"You turned in three lists that night?"

"Every night I'm on."

I handed him the triangle of paper. "Eight o'clock's missing."

"No shit?"

"It doesn't take that long to unclip it. Somebody was in a hurry."

I was looking at him. He stood there holding the torn corner, which was blank on both sides. "Ain't that the night you axed about before?"

"Yeah. I don't guess you make copies."

"Job don't pay that much."

"Uh-huh."

"Hey, I didn't take it."

"The ante just got upped."

His face went wooden. "Fuck you, Jack."

I didn't say anything. He took my two five-dollar bills out of his pocket and threw them on the floor at my feet and reached for the door.

"Take it easy," I said. "It isn't like you called me ahead of the cops to discuss ethics."

He hung there with his hand on the knob. I picked up the bills and held them out. After a moment he took them.

I put the lists back in order and clipped them and rehung the board. Then I switched off the lamp. "Call the police. Don't tell them about the missing list. They'll find out about it in their own time. Leave me clear of it. You never saw me."

He was contemplating the bills, stroking his beard. It didn't mean anything; they were just something to look at. I held out a fifty. He contemplated that.

"I didn't take nothing."

"I believe you. You're too smart to monkey with a murder scene just for a couple of dollars. I had to throw it at you and see if you ducked."

"They lean, I talk," he said. "I got a record."

"For what?"

"They said I stole a car."

"They won't lean that hard. No car thief did this. The fifty's for making them work."

He took it and reached for the telephone. I caught his wrist. "Call from the lobby. All they did was arrest you for a felony. You don't want to be around when they get mad."

"I used that phone to call you."

I let go of him and used the handkerchief on the receiver and buttons. He said, "They'll wonder how come it's clean."

"Not long. Nobody's gone down for prints since the Lindbergh kidnaping."

He went out. I gave him a minute to get down the hall, then went back to Mr. Charm and rummaged inside his coat until I found his slim gray notebook, which I pocketed without opening. Before I left him I picked up a tiny glittering something from the carpet next to his body. It was in shadow from every angle unless you squatted to examine the knife, and I didn't think Lester had done that. In that position it was hard to miss. You don't see that many gold unicorn pins with diamonds for horns. I had seen only one.

10

For the second time I made a call from the telephone at the service station on Tireman. The snow had stopped at five inches and I was standing up to my ankles in someone else's footprints. Just as someone answered, a big party in an arctic cap climbed into a pickup parked by the pumps and turned over the engine with the grinding squeal of a broken starter. I turned my back on the noise and asked for Iris. The pin felt heavy in my pocket.

"Can you receive visitors?" I asked when she came on.

"It's not the House of Corrections," she said. "Did you find my father?"

"I'll be there in ten minutes." The pickup still hadn't started when I pegged the receiver. It sounded like a pig passing a pineapple.

Prostitution rehabilitation centers were out of my experience. I don't know what I expected this one to be like. An old hotel, maybe, or a converted warehouse with a living room setup and a lot of former working girls sitting around in clean cotton shifts with their hair up, reading Bibles. What I found was a middle-size frame house on St. Antoine with cheery yellow siding and flower boxes heaped with snow under the front windows. The bell brought a small short-haired woman in her late thirties, with bright eyes and quick movements that reminded me of a hamster.

"Iris' friend, yes. I'm Mary M." She stuck out a hand and I took it. It was like shaking hands with a small steam wrench.

I stamped snow off my shoes and stepped inside. "What's the M for, Magdalen?"

"Micheljansky. Iris said you were direct. I'll get her."

She pointed me toward an open door off a hallway papered in flowers and hung with photographs of sunsets and took off down it with backless slippers slapping her bare heels. She had on a dragon-red quilted housecoat with white piping and a long blue lacy nightgown under it. The time was almost midnight.

It was clearly a waiting room, only more personal than most. It had an expensive bordered rug and upholstered armchairs and a television set and a glass-topped end table holding up a lamp and some magazines. A blonde in a pink cashmere sweater and white jeans sat curled up in one of the chairs, holding an open book in her lap. Her hair was very light, almost white, and waved back gently from a sweet round face without make-up. She might have been twenty.

I took the chair on the other side of the end table. "I'll guess. *Anna Karenina*."

"Close. *Valley of the Dolls*." She smiled without looking up from the book.

"That's a lot of reading this late."

"I'm not used to sleeping at night."

That was it for conversation. It was forced on my part anyway. After that I sat there waiting and listening to her turn pages. I wanted a cigarette, but there were no ashtrays, which nowadays is supposed to mean something.

"You wouldn't say on the phone if you'd found him."

I looked up. She was wearing a black-and-white-checked blouse tucked into black parachute pants and white half-heel boots that zipped up the sides. Her hair was the way she'd worn it to my office that afternoon. I stood. She saw the blonde and said, "Sara, can we have the room?"

Sara got up and tucked the book under her arm. She was barefoot; her toenails were painted coral. "Another five minutes and I might've been back in business." She smiled at me.

Iris said, "No, you'd be out of business."

"It's like that?"

"No, it isn't."

It was too much for Sara. She left.

"That your type now?" Iris asked.

"To bounce on my knee and tell clean stories to." I found the door and closed it. "I didn't find him. It's about the man who left your mash note."

"You could have left the door open. Mary knows."

"Not all of it."

She sat down then in the chair Sara had been using. I remained standing and unbuttoned my coat. The room was warm. "You reported the break-in to a Mr. Charm?"

"Yes. The name's appropriate."

"To a point. He called me a name and offered to bend my license."

"Not an obscene name. Not Mr. Charm."

"Depends on your definition of obscene, but I didn't start blubbering until he was out of earshot. There's a kid who works at the motel, Lester Hamilton. Maybe you talked to him. Black, goatee, wears his hair like Jimmy Hoffa?"

"I don't think so. The clerk was white."

"Not important. Lester's part of the security, keeps tabs on the cars with plates that aren't in the register. I slipped him ten bucks to check the list for the night you were broken into."

"Bet Mr. Charm won't like it."

"He wasn't doing any complaining when I saw him a little while ago."

She picked up on that. Her face went stiff as dark marble. "He's dead?"

I lit a cigarette and to hell with the no ashtrays. I deposited the match on top of last week's *TV Guide*.

"Somebody put a jackknife where it would do the most good. He didn't take a lot of time finding the right place. In Charm's office. Sometime today between say three and seven. I was there at ten-thirty and it would take at least that long for a body to get cold in a warm room, but not long enough to get stiff."

"Who did it, this Lester?"

"I considered it for about a second and a half. Not for the fifty I gave him to keep me out of it—you too, though I didn't mention you—and if there was something else between them it's not our business. Besides, he called me. Anyone who knows as much about how to knife a man as the one who did Charm also knows that the guy who reports finding the body is always the first suspect. Also I like Lester. But then I've liked killers before."

"Why'd you pay him? I'm clean with the cops."

I tipped some ash onto Richard Chamberlain's forehead and let the opening go past. "This list I asked Lester to get for me was missing from Charm's office, torn off the clipboard in a hurry. I tumbled to the fact that there was a list because I saw Lester making one, but the practice isn't uncommon. Whoever left that drawing in your jewelry box might have thought of it later. Professionals make mistakes sometimes. That's why we fry one every half-century or so.

"What I can't figure is why kill him at all. It's a lot of trouble to go to just to bury a piece of paper that's less than evidence, and of a petty B-and-E to boot. And if our man wanted to drop bodies he'd have started with you instead of drawing skulls and crossbones and shooting innocent automobiles."

"Maybe it was something else like you said."

"Then why steal the list?"

"Maybe the person who killed Charm isn't the same person who took it."

"Maybe. I hate that kind of clutter."

"I see. You want a tidy murder."

It seemed as good a time as any. I took the pin out of my wallet and put it down on the end table with a click. The diamond horn threw off colors under the lamp. "Where were you today between three and seven?"

"Where'd—" She reached automatically for the pin, then withdrew her hand and dropped it in her lap. She curled the other one around it.

"He was almost lying on top of it. Were you with anyone?"

"I was here. Just a minute." She got up and left the room. I extinguished the cigarette in Richard Chamberlain's beard and lit another and smoked that and she came back in. "It's gone."

"I know."

"I didn't lose it in Charm's office. You know that." She was glaring.

"I don't know anything like it. It's not a question of types. We're all killers. The luckiest of us live and die without getting a chance to prove it. Who could have taken it?"

"I don't know. There are no locks on our doors. Mary says they're an encouragement for some of the girls to lock themselves in and carve up their wrists. Amos, I didn't kill him."

"Of course not. It was a pro job and unless there was something more going on than an argument over whether or not your room was burglarized it didn't fit you. Someone wants to scare you back to Jamaica. He's graduated from breaking and entering and property damage to murder and framing, and whoever he is he's been here within the past twenty-four hours. When were you out of your room?"

"Several times. The longest was when I went to see you this afternoon."

"Get out."

"No. Mary's family. Nobody's going to run me out of her place."

"I can't swing police protection. I don't have that kind of drag."

"I wouldn't want it if you could. I saw enough of cops when I was working." She smiled. "A cop who is not a cop is what I want."

I didn't smile back. "Somebody's scared. You're scaring somebody. Scared people with knives and guns scare me. What makes you so frightening?"

"I've gone over it and over it. I can't come up with anything."

"What about that list of johns I asked you to make out?"

"I started to. It's all first names. I can't even put faces to most of them."

"Keep working." I buttoned my overcoat and picked up my hat. "Stay inside as much as you can. Send out for whatever you need, or call me. I'm standing on some evidence to keep the cops off you, so don't worry about them. I'll check in."

She picked up her pin, looked it over on both sides, and put it in one of her pants pockets. "I wish I was paying you."

"I'm flush. It's been a busy winter."

"Yeah, you look it."

We stood listening to the quiet in the room, growing quiet with it. After a long time she took a step toward me and then two more fast and then we kissed.

"Find my father," she said when we came up.

_____

Mary M was in the hall. Iris told her good night and rustled off down it toward the back of the house. A door closed. Mary M regarded me brightly. "Mr. Walker. I thought you'd gone."

"I bet you didn't."

"I don't eavesdrop on my guests' conversations."

"But you do know what goes on in your house."

"Only what the creaks and bangs tell me."

"That's what I'd like to talk to you about," I said.

We went into the room Iris and I had just come out of. Mary M sniffed at the air and wrinkled her nose at the pair of squashed butts on top of the *TV Guide*. Then she turned to face me with her hands in the pockets of her red robe. She had tiny cracks here and there on her face and the kind of roughened complexion that comes from wearing too much harsh make-up too long for too many years. Her eyes were like new pennies in a clear fountain.

"Well, how do you like our little home away from the whorehouse?"

"It's a nice waiting room."

"Nice is what we go for. A lot of our tenants have never known nice. You met Sara?"

"Pretty girl. Is her hair that color?"

"This isn't jail. They can bring whatever chemical beautifiers they want to. Some of them show up at the door with little red wagons. Little red wagons and big black-and-blue shiners. Knife scars sometimes. Sara has one from her collarbone to her left hip. Her business manager caught her moonlighting."

"I guess you get a lot of those."

"We get a lot of those. Some of the others would be in institutions if not here. We've had advanced cases of syphilis with their minds half gone and we get a lot of addicts and not a few reformed addicts who need help staying that way. When we can we get them on programs, but the

73

waiting list is ridiculous. Most of the time I hold their heads."

"Who bankrolls you?"

"Not the United Fund," she said brightly. "Painted whores make rotten poster children. Those who can pay, do. I carry the rest, with help. You'd be surprised how generous some pimps turn out to be when an old retired hooker tells them more about their operations than they know themselves."

"Dangerous."

She tipped back her head and showed all her teeth. "Mister, you diet down to ninety-six pounds and put on a halter and a handkerchief for a skirt and hit Michigan Avenue at two every morning for six years and tell me what's dangerous then." She stopped laughing as suddenly as if a string had broken. "Iris says you're the only white man she'd trust wearing a sheet in a snowstorm. If she's in trouble I want to help."

"You can do that by telling me who's been here since last night that didn't belong."

"Nobody."

"Think," I said. "Especially this afternoon while Iris was out."

"I don't have to think. Nobody was here. If anybody was he'd have seen this." She took her left hand out of its pocket and showed me a square chromed .25 Browning automatic pistol. The light came off it in flat sheets.

I said, "That wouldn't stop a man who thought himself anything of a man."

"Take it away from me."

I reached for it. It wasn't there. An elbow in a scarlet sleeve clipped me on the point of the chin and my teeth snapped together. I moved with the blow and tripped over a bare ankle and upset the lamp on the end table. She spun with a little grunt and feinted at my head with the other elbow. But I saw it for a feint and got a hand around her ankle as her knee came up and pushed her up and over. She turned her shoulder into the fall and rolled on the floor and I stepped in and looked at the pencil-size bore staring up at me from between her palms.

We were like that for a moment, breathing heavily, me standing, she sprawled on her back with her shoulders against the wall and both arms stretched out in front of her ending in the weapon. She had lost a slipper and her robe had come undone. In the cockeyed light of the fallen lamp her tiny nipples stood out against the blue silk of her nightgown.

"Good point," I said.

She showed me her teeth again and lowered the gun. The safety snicked on. "We average two large angry black men a week in wide hats and purple shirts," she said, panting. "I didn't just jump into this venture."

I grinned then and held out a hand. She took it in her steam-wrench grip and sprang up like coiled steel. Pocketing the pistol she went looking for her slipper. Her bare foot was small and narrow and she had a high arch.

"So much for threats from outside." I righted the lamp. "Who's new among your tenants since Iris?"

"She's the latest."

"The reason I'm asking is something was stolen from her room."

She found the slipper and stepped into it. "There is a theft problem here. They don't go out of here angels so I guess it's too much to expect them to come in that way."

"The item turned up. In a place where it shouldn't."

She looked at me, then remembered her robe and closed and tied it, flushing slightly. I liked her for that. An ex-prostitute who can still do you a blush is undefeatable. "I don't suppose you'd tell me where," she said.

"I just met you. First impressions aren't reliable."

"I always went by them." Her bright eyes were steady on me.

I grinned again. "Next time I'll leave my purple shirt at home."

"Come anytime. I promise not to beat you up."

"Mary, that's as romantic a proposition as I ever got."

"Retired cabbies don't give up driving." She saw me out.

11

That night I dreamed I was back in Mr. Charm's office. The view was different: the short-fibered carpet was very close to my face and when I glanced away from it I was looking at the ceiling very far above. It took me a little while to realize I was dead with a knife in my heart. After that I went away from there, and that was when I found out they play trombones in heaven. I awoke into the cold of my bedroom and smoked a cigarette and put it out and turned over and went back to sleep.

In the morning I put on a robe and drank coffee and read Mr. Charm's notebook. It contained a lot of hotel jargon lettered in his neat hand, some of which I understood, and a long section filled with three-digit numbers followed by initials and dollar sums in the low thousands. It excited me a little, if only because house dicks never see that kind of money. Give me a code and I'll break it, but for all I knew, "212, S.M., $5,000" meant that was the going rate for a night with a girl and a whip in room 212. It was the largest amount listed. The rest ran between one and two thousand. I had two cups of coffee over it and gave up for the morning. I thought for a second about giving it to the cops, which fulfilled my citizen's duty that day.

Showered and shaved and dressed in my good gray wool suit, I drove over to the Wayne County Road Commission for a map and to ask directions to a place I had been to a thousand times. The clerk was a helpful young man named Kevin O'Keefe. I thanked him and asked for a card. He gave me one from a little plastic rack on the counter.

The garage where Iris had claimed her fiancé's friend's car was called Park-a-Lot and took up a block of Griswold. It was dank inside and gasoline-smelling and so was the attendant, a beefy white man with dark grease in his fading red hair and a dirty quilted olive-drab coat pulled on over about six shirts. I walked straight up to the glass booth from the entrance and slid O'Keefe's card under the window.

"We got complaints you're letting unauthorized parties park in leased spaces." I ran the words together through the speaking grid as if I'd been saying them all day. "In one case that's happened three times and some of us at County were wondering maybe somebody here's skinning something off on the side."

He read the card, moving his lips, and turned it over with a black thumbnail. Then he looked at me with small colorless eyes crowded close to a blob of a nose like the holes in a bowling ball.

"This here's a private garage. What's County got to do with nothing?"

"Listen, Darrow, anything that's got to do with tires on concrete has got to do with us." I stabbed a finger at him. "This dump is one lonely knob on an iceberg big enough to sink this whole town come next election. I can go back to the office today with some answers or I can send a deputy around with a subpoena and get them Monday in front of the grand jury. You tell me which it is."

He exchanged his tone for one with a whine in it. "Hey, I just work here."

"That's what the stormtrooper told the judges at Nurem-berg."

"Nurm what?"

A green Ford came down the ramp and stopped next to the booth on the other side. The driver gave the at-tendant a bill and he made change. While this was going on I glanced at my watch with an irritated gesture. It had worked once. The car pulled away and he turned back to me.

"What do you need?"

"I got a list of makes and license plate numbers I want you to run and tell me if their owners lease spaces." I hauled out my notebook.

He belched, rumpled his grease-stained hair, belched again, and hoisted a three-ring folder with a stained cloth cover from the shelf under his workspace and opened it. I turned pages in the notebook and fed him some cars and license plate numbers out of the air. He flipped through a fistful of three-by-five cards staggered throughout the folder and grunted negatively while I made marks on the pages. When I mentioned Iris' Malibu and gave him the number he snorted.

"That one we got. Meridian Tours, eighteen hundred Fisher Building. Registered to Dennis Roberts."

"It here?"

He ran a finger along a row of hooks on a board mounted over the opposite window with keys hung on them until he came to an empty one. "It's out."

"Who claimed it?"

"Hell. Ask me what I ate for breakfast last Tuesday. Raleigh might remember. He parks and fetches the per-manents. He's out back on his break."

I took it all down and made up two more cars and num-bers for show. He shook his head. I put away the notebook.

" 'Kay, I'll note your cooperation. Hang on to those records. We might want to subpoena them."

"I got a bad pothole on my block in Redford," he said. "Tore hell out of a brand-new tire. I been waiting six weeks for you guys to come fill it in."

"That's maintenance. Not my department."

"That's what they told the judges at Nurm-whatever," he snarled.

I cut through the building and out the rear entrance on Shelby, where a small slender black party with graying hair and gold-rimmed glasses leaned against the outside wall smoking a cigarette. His clean blue coveralls couldn't have fit him more closely if they were tailored and he had on high-tops freshly blacked and laced as tight as a Victorian lady's corset. He looked to be in his late forties.

Looking at him I abandoned the road commission ploy — the attendant inside had my only card anyway — and handed it to him straight on. "Raleigh?"

He came away from the building with a kind of easy grace you don't normally associate with small men and took the cigarette from his mouth, flicking ash onto the sidewalk. "Me." He had confident eyes behind the glasses.

I showed him my ID. "Client of mine claimed a car here a few days ago, yellow Chevy Malibu." I gave him the license plate number.

"Yeah."

"Yeah means what?"

"Means a client of yours claimed a car here. Fine young ginger-colored thing. Big eyes."

"That's her. You've got a good memory."

"Only for the important things."

I stretched a five-dollar bill between my hands. "You were the first to find out she was in town. Who'd you tell?"

"Save your money, mister."

"You won't say?"

"It worth five bucks to you to hear me say I didn't tell no one?"

"It might be, if you meant it."

He held out his palm then and I laid the bill in it. He unzipped a coverall pocket and folded the bill inside and zipped it closed. Then he took another drag.

"I didn't tell no one. I see pretty ladies every day."

I left it at that. I wanted to believe him. It's worth five dollars to meet an honest car hop.

The Fisher is a junior Empire State Building soaring in fluted Art Deco splendor from a parapeted base, Albert Kahn's bold reply to the glass boxes that would eventually smother his art. Three stories of marbled arcade run the length of its base, with room down the center to display everything from antique cars standing on spotless rubber inside velvet ropes to the history of fashion from goatskins to chinchilla wraps. I rode the elevator up the tower to the eighteenth floor and stepped out into a blue-carpeted reception area where an East Indian girl seated behind the desk told me that Mr. Roberts was vacationing in the South of France for six weeks, would I care to speak with someone else?

I rode back down and chipped the frost off my windshield and drove to the office, where a gray Lincoln Town Car was parked in front of the entrance with its motor purring.

You couldn't miss it. In a city full of brown slush and rusted tailpipes it looked fresh out of the crate, polished to a high soft gloss with a full set of those tinted windows that are almost always bad news for someone in my profession. I parked down the street and got my gun out of the glove compartment and checked the load and put it inside the right-hand pocket of my overcoat before getting out. I'm not a Communist. People with nice clothes and spotless cars aren't automatically my enemies. I just don't like them parking in front of running-down buildings in the middle-rent district on cold February days without going inside; especially not a building where I happen to have my office. I crossed the street to that side and started walking.

I had the timing figured right. I was abreast of the right rear fender when the front door on the passenger's side opened and a medium-size Oriental climbed out. He was a gawky case in a tan double-breasted suit that fit him like aluminum siding and eight inches of neck sticking out of his collar. He had an egg-shaped head cropped closely and badly, as if with hedge trimmers, and black hooded eyes in a face the color of rotten teeth. His upper lip was as long as a monkey's.

I had picked my spot with my back to the building and my hand on the gun in my pocket. The Oriental stopped coming. He stood in the slush in shiny brown hand-lasted shoes small enough for a woman to wear, with his bony wrists hanging four inches out of his cuffs and nothing in his hands. The car door was open behind him. I could see the driver's leg and an arm supported on the cushioned rest between the seats, both sheathed in powder-blue serge.

The tinted rear window whispered down. A smooth round brown face like a cocoa moon looked out at me and a hand grasped the collar of the man sitting next to him and yanked him forward so he could look too. This was Raleigh, the parking attendant at the garage on Griswold. "Thees him?" asked Moon Face. Raleigh nodded. "Hokay, get out." Moon Face shoved him back against the door on the other side.

Raleigh clawed it open and looked at me again over the Lincoln's roof with one foot on the curb. He straightened his gold-rimmed glasses. "Nothing personal."

I shrugged and he slammed the door and began walking. I never saw him again.

"Get een," said Moon Face.

82

I laughed at him.

"Ang."

The Oriental's monkey mask twisted, the long lip pulling away from teeth that made his complexion look less rotten. Air hissed in through his nose and he went into a crouch with his left foot planted before his right and his left fist thrust out in front of him at shoulder height and his right cocked at his waist, knuckles foremost.

I rolled back the hammer on the gun in my pocket. It made a crisp statement in the cold air. The Oriental held his position.

A young couple in dress overcoats came down the sidewalk and slowed as they neared us. The woman put a gloved hand on the man's arm and they picked up their pace. We let them pass between us.

"Why you dicking aroun'? Heet him!"

Moon Face hadn't heard the noise of the hammer. I said, "Maybe he knows if he moves I'll turn him into a Chinese checkerboard."

"Hey, chamaco, no guns. Just talk."

"Call off your Pekingese."

"Ang."

Ang lowered his hands and relaxed his stance. His face went slack and dumb. I let down the hammer gently. The black eyes glittered.

"Hokay, chamaco, get een."

"I can hear you from here."

Moon Face spat a string of breakneck Spanish and got out of the car. He was a five-foot butterball in a white felt hat with a red silk band and a brim that swept down on one side Capone fashion. He had on a pearl-gray alpaca coat with a thick fur collar over a maroon three-piece suit and a white cashmere scarf, and when one of his yellow pumps sank to its top in slush he used some more Spanish. On the sidewalk he stooped and wiped off the shoe carefully with a rose-colored silk handkerchief. Then he tossed the handkerchief in the gutter.

"You see that, chamaco?" he said. "Twenny dollars an' tax, I t'row it away 'cause it's dirty. How much you worth, five-six t'ousan', less?"

"I'm not dirty." I kept my hand in my pocket.

"Man says he's not dirty, you hear that, Felipe?"

"I heard, Manolo." This was the driver, leaning over a little now and showing me his long grave brown Latin face and high bald dome. He looked Castilian, a contrast to his boss, who looked digger Mexican, round and greasy, a wallet-size Fatty Arbuckle with protruding eyes and a small mouth with a pouty lower lip that made his face look broader than it already was.

"Hombre, they find you in a sewer pipe, you be dirty. Ang there he done a man in Seoul with just his head. That's why he's here."

"Remind me not to rub it for luck."

" 'Course, that man he didn' have a gun like you. Karate, judo, tae kwan do, they been doing that what, couple t'ousan' years? Man blow them off with a piece he bought for fi'teen dollars in a crapper. 'S'why I rounded out Ang some. Show the man."

The Korean reached in the side pocket of his tan coat and I tightened my grip on the gun. He saw that but didn't react. He came out with a jackknife and flipped it open by the blade, then somersaulted it and closed his fingers on the handle. The blade had been ground needle-thin.

"You can empty that piece into him, he still cut off your head. He would, too. These yellow boys they're loyal. I'd hire more only a man's got a responsibility to his own people." He blew into his hands and rubbed them together. They were puffy and soft-looking, like brown dough. "Well, chamaco, what we going to do with you?"

"For starters you can stop calling me chamaco."

"You know what it means?"

"It's a bastardized word for boy. The kind of boy that black men get called sometimes."

He buttoned his overcoat and tucked the ends of the scarf inside the lapels. The cold was getting to him.

"Tell your girlfriend go home, hombre. Tell her Sam said Detroit is no place to be in the winter. Or the spring or the summer or the fall. Tell her the island's better for her health."

"I thought your name was Manolo."

He held out a hand and the Korean laid the knife in it. Then he leaned in through the open door on the passenger's side and tore the blade across the leather front seat in a long arc. Foam rubber bulged obscenely out. Felipe watched the operation with a sad expression. Moon Face turned back to face me and folded the knife.

"You see that, chamaco? An' I *like* thees car."

He returned the knife to Ang and got back into the rear seat, stepping over the slush. He reached for the door handle. "Tell her, hombre. Then maybe you take a little vacation yourself. You look tired." He pulled the door shut and hummed up the window.

Ang remained for a beat, his black eyes on me, then pocketed the knife and backed away a step and spun on the ball of his foot, bending himself into the ruined front seat. The car was already in motion when he got the door closed. I had no trouble getting the license plate. It read GRANDE.

I pried my fingers loose of the gun and went inside.

12

The morning *Free Press* was waiting for me inside the mail slot among the daily junk. I scooped it all up automatically. Automatically I unlocked the inner office door and I automatically gave the mail a burial at sea in the wastebasket. I poured myself two fingers automatically from the bottle in the file drawer of the desk and drank both of them and after that I started thinking again. No thoughts worth an award. I considered that foam rubber spilling out of slashed upholstery has the same effect as bloody entrails.

I called police headquarters and asked for Lieutenant Thaler's extension. It was busy. I cradled the receiver and went through the newspaper. Mr. Charm's murder had made the lower right-hand corner of the front page, with a picture of the bagged corpse being wheeled out the side door and no mention of the motel's name anywhere in the article. Charm, first name Eldon, had been discovered by an employee who also wasn't named. I didn't appear and neither did the fact of the missing list. It was a very short article. Acting Lieutenant Leonard Hornet, in charge of the investigation, said that robbery had not been ruled out as a motive.

The man who finally answered Mary Ann Thaler's line said she wasn't at her desk. I thanked him and hung up and drove down. Before going inside I transferred the revolver from my coat pocket to the glove compartment. It was legal but I didn't care to have the fine print on my permit read while the metal detectors were clanging.

There were more detectives on hand at that time of day, but the more of them there are the quieter things get, somehow. I found Thaler in conversation with a plain-clothesman in the squad room, half sitting on the edge of a cluttered desk with her ankles crossed and her arms folded. They were trim ankles above cut-down brown loafers and she was wearing a red skirt and a blue metallic blouse and a gray jacket. The blouse brought out the blue in her eyes behind the tortoiseshell glasses. The plain-clothesman was two hundred eighty pounds of hard fat in black polyester pants whose cuffs dragged at his heels and a burgundy blazer with brass buttons and anchors. His short red necktie brought out the congestion in his face. I knew him as Sergeant Hornet, John Alderdyce's second whip in Homicide.

"Who the hell let you in here?" His features were spread all over his raw slab of a face.

"Good morning, Sergeant. Have you had your breakfasts today?"

"Acting Lieutenant, damn you."

"I bet you can pull it off. You've been acting like a detective for years."

He glared at Thaler. "You got business with this horse's ass?"

"He's part of the public we serve," she said. "Is there anything else I can help you with, Leonard?"

He mumbled a negative and gave me the hard look before rolling back toward Alderdyce's office.

"He hates the name Leonard." She looked at me. "I'm

still waiting on that ballistics report, if that's what you're here for."

"Just partly. Got a minute?"

She glanced down at a man's gold watch on her wrist. It was the only thing mannish about her. "Just about that."

We went into her office, where she offered me a cup of coffee and I accepted it. The flowers had been changed; other than that the place looked the same as it had the day before, no less tidy.

"Is that the motel murder you're working on with Hornet?" I asked.

She poured a cup for herself. She had real china cups, not Styrofoam, with matching saucers. "Peripherally. It looks more like some kind of mob thing now than robbery. Hornet liked the employee, Hamilton, at first—liked him a lot—but it won't hang without a motive."

"What made anyone think robbery?"

"The safe in the office had been jimmied. But we found six thousand in receipts still inside. Whatever the killer was after, it wasn't money."

"Just six thousand?"

"It's an overnight stop, not the Westin. What did you want to talk about?"

I sat down, balancing my cup and saucer. "With John on leave you're my only friendly face in the department. I was wondering if you had anything on file on a fat little Hispanic who dresses like Al Capone and glides around in a gray Lincoln with a plate that reads GRANDE." I spelled it. "He calls himself Sam, but his driver calls him Manolo. Has a Korean torpedo named Ang, a real Bruce Lee type."

"Manuel Malviento."

"That came out fast."

She remained standing beside the desk and sipped coffee and placed the cup in its saucer, holding them in front of her. She didn't look anything at all like an old maid in a parlor. "He's managed to rub up against every detail in the department except Rape and I've got money in the pool says he'll do that by next Monday. He came up from Colombia in the crowd five years ago and started with dope and now he's got a thumb on every dirty dollar in town. He calls himself Sam Mozo. *Mozo*, that's young man in Spanish. He's twenty-four. How'd you come to step in that?"

"He's threatening a client."

"The lady with the bullet?"

I said it was.

"Hide her good. That little creep's a stone killer."

"So far he's just talking."

"Two years ago he was just another mule running kilos for the big boys. He's got one prior for possession for sale, one-year probation. Six months ago Jackie Acardo disappeared, and here comes Sam Mozo out from behind a bush to pick up the pieces. Acardo was the last goombah hanging fire against the Colombians in the dope trade here. He didn't just go on vacation. The Acardos would be moving on Mozo only he's just one of a couple of dozen vest-pocket godfathers who have benefited from Jackie's powder and this generation of mobsters likes to look before it breaks out the blowtorches."

I drank coffee and listened.

"We had Mozo down here once for threatening an undercover officer. He took off his own thousand-dollar pink cashmere coat and cut it to ribbons with a jackknife in front of the cop, by way of showing how little anything means to him. He likes to destroy nice things."

"That's him. Someone ought to take him down while he still has some possessions left. What's his connection to the Park-a-Lot Garage on Griswold?"

"He probably owns it. Parking garages and auto dealerships are how he launders his money. Also they pay almost as well as cocaine and heroin. You ever store a car in this town for any length of time?" She arranged a blank arrest form on the desk for a coaster and set down her cup and saucer. "The feds would like to take him down, or at least deport him, but he finagled citizenship somehow, and Immigration is a mess. Don't laugh at him too hard. You'll still be laughing when he slides a knife between your ribs."

I busied myself lighting a cigarette so as not to meet her gaze. I knew what was in it. She straightened with her fingers splayed on the desk.

"You were pretty interested in that motel killing just now," she said. "Do you figure Sam Mozo for it?"

"An hour ago I never heard of Sam Mozo."

"Yes." She went on looking at me. Her eyes were as hard as baby blue ever gets. "I just got a glimpse at how come you're so short on friendly faces down here."

I got up and put my cup and saucer next to hers. "I'll be available whenever those test results come in. Thanks again for running them."

She took her hands off the desk. "If it were my case I'd be turning you on the spit now."

"I bet you can turn it, too. But it's Hornet's barbecue and you don't like him any more than I do."

"Don't trade on that. Just because I'm female doesn't mean I'm not in the brotherhood."

"I'll remember."

"And watch out for Sam Mozo. He only *looks* ridiculous."

I took myself out. I had a column of ash growing and hers was the only floor in the place I didn't feel comfortable using for a tray.

13

Ump," said a tired male voice on the other end of the line.

"Sorry?"

"UMMP. What do you need?"

There was no background noise in the Detroit office of United Musicians and Musical Performers. I pictured a clothes closet with a view of the air shaft and a bald man in rolled-up shirtsleeves sitting at a desk that had come over in steerage with Cortez. Aloud I said, "I'm booking a wedding reception. I need to find a trombonist named George Favor."

"Sounds like a real hip wedding. How about an accordion?"

"No, I want Favor."

"What's his card number?"

"If I knew that I'd probably know his address."

He put down the receiver and I listened for a few minutes to a chair squawking and someone's thumb flicking through cards in a file. I snapped a shred of pencil eraser off my blotter.

"No George Favor," said the voice. "I got a Partee Favor,

that's two *e*'s in 'Partee.' Maybe you want her for the bach-
elor blowout the night before."

"Not for this groom. Maybe you misplaced Favor's card.
He was sitting in at the Kitchen as recently as three years
ago."

"Says who?"

"Joe Wooding, for one."

"Sweet Joe? He should talk."

"Sorry?"

"Nothing. I talked out of turn."

"No, I need to know if he's any kind of a source."

"It's just that they were still using him as a textbook case
when I came on here. It's against union rules to perform
free for anything but charity benefits and he was blowing
bass and horn gratis all over town. The union yanked his
card several times and finally didn't give it back. Sweet Joe
Wooding. You sure he isn't dead?"

I reassured him. "Maybe he just liked to play."

"Then he should've locked himself in his bedroom and
put on a command performance for the wallpaper. You
offer your talent for free, pretty soon they think that's all
any musician's worth. Bad all around."

"What do you play?"

"Pinochle."

I gave him that one. "Got anything on a female vocalist
named Glen Dexter? She used to sing with Favor."

He flipped through some more cards. "Dexter, nope."

"Try Edwina. That's her niece."

"No Dexters."

I stopped talking to him and got out the metropolitan
directory. There was only one Edwina Dexter listed in
Ypsilanti. I dialed it and got a throaty voice on a recording
and a number in Detroit for emergencies. I stretched the
definition and tried that. A man answered.

"Sound Management."

"Edwina Dexter, please."

"Wye?"

"What makes it your business?"

"No, I mean Wye Dexter."

"Because that's her name."

"Wye's what we call her," he said patiently. "Second."

I waited several. Abbott and Costello would have had fun with the telephone conversations I'd been having lately. The voice came back on.

"She's recording right now. Can I take a message?"

"Where are you located?"

"East Grand at Mack. Big cinderblock building with the name out front. You can't miss it."

I didn't. It had almost no windows and a small paved parking lot with three cars in it. I banged on a big blank steel door. A man in faded jeans and a plaid flannel shirt opened it and looked me over. He had white hair in bangs and glasses on top of his head and was at least thirty years too old for that look.

"I'm here to see Edwina Dexter," I said.

"Wye?"

I recognized his voice. "You won't get me with that one again."

"You're the one who called. Listen, she's still in the booth, but she'll be breaking soon. You can come in and sit if you're quiet."

They hadn't done anything with the place except haul in a lot of electronic equipment and some used furniture to sit on. The walls and floor were bare concrete and nobody was going broke heating the place. I kept on my hat and coat — no one had offered to take them anyway — and followed him between rows of reel recorders and knobbed panels to a sofa with a loose tasseled cover and sat down. Placing a finger to his lips, he walked on thick-soled sneakers to a row of stools at a tilted control board and took one. The others were occupied by a younger man and woman wearing earphones. They all shared the same tailor.

From where I sat I could see them and a partitioned-off room across from them with a big window, behind which a woman sat speaking into the microphone attached to her headset. From time to time she lifted a hand to turn pages in a looseleaf notebook propped on a music stand in front of her. She was broadcasting into the rest of the building in the throaty voice I'd heard on her telephone recording and it took me a few minutes to realize she was reading Dickens. Compared to what I'd been speaking lately it was a foreign language.

After ten minutes or so the aging campus radical at the control board called for a break. The woman in the booth stretched, arching her back, and took off the headset. She had short black hair and wore a man's denim workshirt with white stitching. From a little distance she might have been a man, but I'd seen her stretch. I got up and went over and tapped on the door.

"It's open."

She was lighting a cigarette off a disposable butane lighter. Her legs were long in rose-petal jeans and fringed knee-length buckskin boots hooked under the rung of her stool the way no man can stand to sit for more than thirty seconds. She was about thirty-five and slim, not quite wiry. She would be too tall for wiry. I had her figured for not much under six feet.

"Honk if you see something you like," she said.

I'd been looking at her for ten seconds. "Sorry. I thought you'd be older."

"I get that from bartenders. They think asking for my ID puts them halfway home. Who are you?"

"My name's Walker. I'm a private investigator looking for George Favor. Your aunt knew him."

"I guess so. He killed her."

The room contained two stools, an upright piano, the music stand, and a bare yellow oak table with the headset lying on it. I nodded at that. "That live?"

"I unplugged it." She flicked some ash onto the floor without taking her eyes off me. They were hazel. She had a square jaw and rouge on her cheeks in two stripes as if she'd dipped a thumb in the pot and streaked them on her way out the door. They were already as high as an Indian's. I hooked the other stool with an ankle and threw a leg over it.

"*Great Expectations*," she said, tipping her head toward the open notebook on the stand. "Story of my life. I wanted to sing like Aunt Glen, but nobody wants to hear that stuff now and anyway I never had her talent. So I'm reading hacked-up classics for people who are too lazy to turn pages."

"Isn't that one narrated by a boy?"

"Someone thought it would go over bigger if it's read by a woman with a borderline sexy voice. It'll sell like a brick anyway; no car chases. Is the old man in trouble?"

"Not unless what you said is true."

"First time I said it out loud. Now that I have I can hear how stupid it is. It's true, though, in a way."

I got out a cigarette.

She said, "Aunt Glen had real talent, not like me. She could have been as big as Ella or Doris Day. Things were loosening up in the fifties and it wouldn't have hurt her that she'd been recording with a black band. But getting hooked up with a black musician was fatal."

"That what you meant by killing her?"

"No, I meant it literally. Well, sort of. The singing didn't mean that much to her. Not as much as marrying and raising a family. That was okay then for a woman, nobody sneered at you for it. Times weren't as enlightened. Anyway they were going to be married, and then they split up. I found out later it was because George refused to give her children.

"Glen was my father's sister. She spoiled me pretty rotten whenever she came to visit. I can still see her, wearing white cotton gloves and one of those Robin Hood hats with a pheasant feather in it and bringing some expensive present for me, something I'd begged my parents for and been refused. She always knew. She was a beautiful woman and she loved children, I mean *loved* them. I'd see her watching me, and young as I was I could feel her wishing I was hers. When George told her it wasn't going to happen it destroyed her. She spent the next ten years looking for a man who would give her what she wanted and who she cared for. By the time she found one it was too late. The doctors told her it could be dangerous at her age. Of course she didn't listen. She had a stroke. Several strokes."

I put some ash on the floor. I heard it land.

"They tried to save the baby," she said, "put her on life support until she'd reached full term, but they weren't as good at that then; they lost it too. It was a boy." She rubbed her eyes. "Smoke. Well, I've hated George ever since, because if she'd had a kid when she first wanted one there wouldn't have been any problems. Stupid. I didn't know him at all, went to one or two places with my parents where Aunt Glen was appearing with him and met him once backstage. I remember being fascinated by his shiny trombone. Who hired you to look for him?"

I hesitated. "His daughter."

She was silent for a long time, looking at me. Then she remembered the cigarette between her fingers and took a long pull. She blew out smoke. "The son of a bitch."

"By all accounts it wasn't planned. Chances are he doesn't even know he's a father. I was hoping you'd know where he is so I could tell him."

"I haven't seen him since I was seven. Who told you about me?"

"L. C. Candy. He said he met you last year at Montreux."

"I remember. He played 'Yesterday Blues' note-for-note the way George used to. It wasn't the same without Glen singing. I always thought whatever success he had he owed to her."

"It was a tough life even then."

"I'd take it. I was pregnant once. I fixed it. Even if having a kid doesn't kill you straight off it does in the end. As soon as you have one your life is over. Don't have children and you'll never die, that's my philosophy." She smashed out the butt against the table and let it drop. "Some sense of humor God has. He gave Glen a voice but she wanted to be a mother. He gave me the chance to be one but I wanted to sing. Neither of us got what we wanted. I bet the bastard's laughing."

"You ready to go again, Wye?" The white-haired man's voice sounded deeper over the speaker above the window. He had a microphone in front of him on the control board.

She put on the headset and plugged it in. I got off my stool. I thanked her, but she was looking over the pages on the stand and didn't hear me, or acted like she didn't. As I left the building, Pip was making the acquaintance of the convict in the cemetery.

That was the file on Little Georgie Favor as far as I could take it. The rest was filling out Social Security forms and driver's license replacement applications and waiting for civil service to report back, and unless he drove or collected retirement benefits he was smoke. Detroit is a big city in a big country. Being black and old in Detroit is like being young and homosexual in San Francisco. Even a needle in a haystack glitters.

I fed two dimes to a black bandit on East Grand and punched out a number from memory. Mary M answered.

"Hey, karate," I said.

She hesitated, but only for a second. "This sounds like Mr. Walker."

I complimented her on her quickness and asked for Iris. When she came on I started in first.

"I haven't found him. Are you free this morning?"

"I never was."

"Very funny."

"I was planning to see the Rivera exhibit at the DIA."

"Alone?"

"Apparently not." Her tone was dry.

"A little culture won't kill me. Twenty minutes okay?"

"Is it about—that thing?"

"Only partly. It's about Favor too."

"Twenty's fine."

14

A schizophrenic structure, the Detroit Institute of Arts, with an arched Italian Renaissance central portion carved from white marble in 1927 and essentially blank gray granite wings stuck on the back forty-four years later. I found Iris upstairs in front of a modern primitive mural, done in pastels and earth tones, of factory workers with tortured faces and straining tendons. Canvases staggered the walls showing colored dandies and sweating trumpet players and naked women peeping through bushes of fat green leaves. They reminded me of Iris. The woman herself was wearing the yellow beret and tan coat over last night's pants and boots. She had her arm through the strap of a shoulderbag big enough for the gun I knew she had inside it and the Third Armored Division.

"He had strength." She was looking at the mural.

"Came by it honestly," I said. "You don't paint men at hard labor like that out of anatomy class. Were you followed here?"

"I don't think so."

"Then you probably were. I like what he does with perspective." A man in a brown homburg and black coat and flowing white moustache had paused in front of the painting.

When he moved on, Iris said: "What about my father?"

"I just talked to the woman who could have been his niece. That would have made her your cousin, only it didn't happen that way and so you're strangers."

"Am I supposed to understand that?"

"No. I've done all that sleuthing can. Now we wait a month or six weeks for the bureaucracy to get back to me. I know he did a little playing at the Kitchen up until about three years ago. After that he drops out the bottom of the picture. Implication is he's dead. He wasn't that well."

"He's not dead."

"Okay."

A short-haired boy and girl in matching camouflage jackets joined us, holding hands. The boy swept his other hand here and there on the painting explaining this and that and the girl listened and then told him he was full of organic fertilizer. They drifted off arguing.

"What makes him alive?" I asked.

"You don't go twenty years thinking your father's dead and then find out he wasn't your father and then start looking for your real father and find out he's dead too. Keep looking."

"When you make that much sense it's hard not to."

She smiled then. A schoolteacher with orange hair and a gaggle of brats in smelly coats and knit caps started cheeping around the mural and we crossed to one of the long-backed nudes. The teacher would avoid that.

"I can go back and turn over some old ground. It won't do anything but you never know."

"I'll pay you when I have money."

"Forget money. You're hung up on money. If you gave me money right now I'd give it to a guard and ask him to clear the culture-soakers out of the place so we can talk. What are you to Sam Mozo?"

"Sam Mozo." She was looking at the nude.

"Right name Manuel Malviento. Dope and parking garages. A little toad with a big hat and a bodyguard straight out of Sax Rohmer. He said, 'Tell your girlfriend Sam said Detroit is no place to be in the winter.' Or any other season. He likes to carve things up. Cars. Coats. Night managers. He's hard to forget."

"I didn't say I didn't know him."

"Old customer, pimp, what?"

"Husband."

The man in the homburg was standing in front of the painting next to ours. We moved over one. It was a portrait of a slouch-hatted Negro with a cigarette burning between his fingers.

"Ex, actually," she said. "We were married about a week."

"I'm surprised it lasted that long."

"He was this fat little spick flat off the banana boat, knew about six words in English and three of them were 'mama.' He picked me up in a dive on the river and we went across the street to this roach trap of a hotel. They're gone now, both buildings; towers five and six of the RenCen ate 'em up. He offered me five hundred to marry him for six weeks. I looked at his roll and I looked at him and I said make it a thousand and we'll get divorced in the morning."

"I'm starting to see."

"We settled on six hundred and a week. He wasn't sure about how long it would take to be considered valid but he hoped that would do it. We got the license and he brought in some greasy little minister with beer breath and a mail-order divinity degree, all legal, and we did it right there in the room. I guess we had a honeymoon for a couple of hours. I was high as taxes."

"That's what it would take."

"I never thought about him after the divorce went through until you mentioned him just now," she said. "I never saw him again after that night. Our wedding night."

"When did all this happen?"

"Before I got straight. Three, four years ago."

"You should've stuck with him. You'd be in furs now, provided he didn't get miffed and turn them into pillow stuffing. You too."

"What's that mean?"

"Your ex-husband is pulling a long shadow these days. He's got a trade and a maroon suit. Blowing his nose in rose-colored silk."

"You said dope?"

"You'd think he invented it. He also owns the garage where you picked up the car you're using. The attendant who brought it around remembered you. Did you sign for it with your own name?"

"Yes. I forgot about that."

"You wouldn't have if I'd remembered to ask. Either Mozo saw your signature or someone did who knew about your arrangement and told him. Half an hour after I spoke to the attendant, the man himself was waiting for me outside my building with a Korean killer and a driver named Felipe. That's when he gave me the message."

"He's the one who's after me?"

"I didn't ask. There didn't seem to be any point."

"What's he got against me? He paid me and I delivered. I don't—"

The room was filling up. I closed a hand around her upper arm and took her through the arch into the next room, which was nearly deserted. We swept past the man in the homburg, who was admiring a porcelain vase on a marble stand with his hands folded behind his back. We found an empty corner.

"Mozo married an American citizen so he could stay in this country," I said. "You. Only if the feds can prove it was a marriage of convenience they can revoke his new citizenship and deport him in a hot Colombian minute. Three years ago they wouldn't have bothered, but he's festered some since then. He's trafficking big and he probably killed Jackie Acardo for the green light. Say you're Sam Mozo and you find out that the weekend wife who can put you on the next plane to Bogotá is suddenly back in town. What would you do?"

"You're crushing my arm."

I'd forgotten I was still gripping it. I let go. A lip got bitten.

"If I'm such a threat, how come he's playing games? If he or one of his people could get into my motel room, why'd they pick a time when I wasn't there and leave a note instead of just doing me? Why put a bullet in my car when I'm not in it?"

"I didn't think to ask him," I said. "I had a building at my back and Number One Son waving an Arkansas toothpick under my nose. Maybe he doesn't kill women. Maybe his mother was one and he's got a jelly spot for them. More likely the heat's still too high from the Acardo job and if he can flush you out of town instead of killing you he will. With position comes diplomacy."

"That doesn't figure if he killed Mr. Charm."

"I didn't say I had it all worked out."

She said, "I had a seventy-five-dollar-a-day habit. It was six hundred dollars for a couple of hours' work."

"Nobody's blaming you for surviving. Question is, how do we keep it up? Mozo's running out of car seats to slash."

"I'm not leaving Mary M's."

"There's a rat in the woodwork there."

"It's woodwork I know."

"Would the world fall off its axis if you went back to

Jamaica until Mozo gets dusted off by the law, or more likely by his own kind?"

Her face took on the fired hardness of an Egyptian sculpture. "I came here to find my father. I can't do that from Kingston if you're going to give it up."

"You could go to the feds. When they find out what you've got you'll have more bodyguards than you ever had johns."

"You said yourself bodyguards are just nightlights."

"They beat total darkness."

"True. And after I testify they'll change my name and give me a wheat field in Nebraska to hide in. Feds are just cops with tailors."

I peered into a glass case full of medieval knives. The blades didn't look much more drawn than my reflection. "If I keep on looking, will you go home?"

"I'll go back to Mary M's and wait to hear something."

"That isn't the deal."

"You can keep it then. People my father's age die while people my age are trying to book seats on airplanes to the States."

"You'll stay put. I mean grow roots."

She thought about it a second, then nodded.

"I hate bargaining with ex-hookers."

She laughed. I'd forgotten the sound of it.

"I'll follow you back." I touched her elbow and we turned toward the exit. The man in the gray homburg was standing in front of it.

He swept off the hat with a gesture that the novelists call courtly and inclined his head a fraction of an inch. He was my height and bald to the crown, from where his hair hung straight and snow-white down the back of his head to his collar. The moustache was waxed lightly so that the tips turned up and there were deep humor lines around his faded brown eyes. He looked like a Mediterranean

Buffalo Bill. "Mr. Walker?" His voice was pleasantly deep with the accent set in it like a precious stone.

I said nothing and waited for the other shoe to drop. Iris' arm tightened, trapping my hand between it and her ribcage.

"I am Tomaso Acardo," the man said. "My nephew would like some words with you if you have time."

15

What words?"

"That's entirely up to Francisco. I am not actively involved in the family enterprise. It was my brother's wish."

At this point we were sharing the room with the young couple who had argued about the mural and a workman in gray coveralls replacing a lightbulb in one of the display cases. Our voices carried. I lowered mine.

"Last I heard Frankie Acardo was doing a nickel in Jackson on a stolen credit card rap."

"One to three," corrected Tomaso. "He was released in December after fourteen months. The entire affair was a miscarriage of justice."

"It miscarries a lot. Look at the shape it's in. Where is he now?"

"The Adelaide Hotel. Do you know it?"

"What's Frankie A doing in a dump like the Adelaide?"

"His father owned it. Owns it. He worked—works out of the eighth floor. Francisco is using it until he returns."

"It doesn't sound like you think he's going to."

"There comes a point after which you must force yourself to hope. A car is waiting."

"Mine too. Acardo back seats have a bad habit of coming back empty."

The moustache bent down slightly, but the eyes remained humorous. They had the look of eyes that had seen most of what they had seen from outside. "The invitation is extended in good faith. The lady is welcome as well."

"The lady's on her way home." I squeezed her elbow for silence; she had started to squirm. "I'll see her there. Maybe I'll come around after that. These are working hours."

"Francisco requested me to tell you that you won't be out anything for the inconvenience."

"I laugh at money. How much am I laughing at?"

He laughed himself. It was a deep, quiet rumble that turned all of the heads in the room not engraved in marble. It must have been something to hear when he took the lid off at weddings and wakes. "You're impertinent," he said. "I was known for that myself when I was younger."

"Is that why you're not actively involved in the family enterprise?"

"As I recall it had a very great deal to do with the decision." He stopped laughing. "I own quarries, Mr. Walker. Our father, Giovanni's and mine, gave me my first and now I have twenty. Undoubtedly a number of the sculptures in this room came from my stone. That first quarry was intended as an insult, a symbol of my father's disappointment, rather in the way that parents of my generation used to leave lumps of coal in the stockings of ill-behaved children. Have you checked the price of coal lately, Mr. Walker?"

"So how come you're running errands?"

"My name is still Acardo. My nephew is new to authority and a mistake on his part would brand me as thoroughly. There has been at least one federal agent parked outside my house since I was forty."

———

"Did he follow me here too?"

"I think I will leave that to Francisco to explain." He put on his homburg, cocking it an eighth of an inch over his right eye. "Shall I tell him to expect you?"

"I get down to that neighborhood sometimes."

"Sometime today would be to your advantage."

He touched his hat and left us then, his custom shoes making no noise at all on the carpeted floor.

"What was that all about?" Iris asked.

"Jackie Acardo's brother." I let go of her elbow. "Looks like son Frank agrees with the cops about Sam Mozo dusting his old man. So far I haven't had anything to do with the Acardos, just with your ex."

"I wish you'd stop calling him that. It isn't as if we picked out a silver pattern together. You're not going."

"It isn't every day you get an Acardo invitation without guns."

"Our deal's not even dry yet. You're supposed to be looking for my father."

"You won't need a father if you're dead. Sam Mozo wants you that way if he can't have you out of town, and the Acardos want Sam Mozo. It's a question of priorities."

"You don't know they want any part of him. His name didn't even come up."

"I'll know after I talk to Frank."

Her eyes were large on me, coffee brown with the pupils wide. "There's more to it. You're up to something."

I put on an innocent look. It went over like the two-dollar bill. Rivera wouldn't have painted it and the DIA wouldn't have hung it. I saw her back home. All that art was making me feel out of my depth.

Automobile money had put up the Adelaide, back when taxes were a democratic joke and red brick came five dollars the hundredweight. The brick was stained now, the canopy out front pigeon-striped and fraying, but the vaulted lobby was big enough to park a fleet of trucks inside and the old leather chairs and sofa had been redone recently in dark green Naugahyde. The ferns had fronds as big as Volkswagens. A wet snow was falling outside; as I paused to wipe my feet six pairs of eyes watched me above newspapers. Among the men seated in the chairs, the FBI agents were easy to distinguish from the local muscle. The local muscle wore hats.

The clerk behind the marble reservation desk was a big shale-eyed man who looked like a bartender. The shale eyes moved behind me when I asked for the number of Frank Acardo's room and two of the men who had been reading when I came in joined me. They had on narrow-brimmed hats and light topcoats open over three-piece suits and striped neckties, one red and silver, the other gray and white. Gray-and-White was a redhead with freckles on his face and hands and an upswung Irish nose. He was my height. The other was a shade shorter with ears that stuck out from hairless temples and I knew from them that from there on up he was as bald as a bearing. His eyebrows were thin and so fair that at first they looked as if he'd shaved them too. His mouth was a straight lipless line like a coin slot.

They were killers. You'll hear that it's in their eyes, but eyes don't kill people; the redhead's were merry-looking, in fact. It was in their plumb-steady posture and in the way their neat clean short-nailed hands hung in front of their thighs with the fingers bent slightly, and it was in the way you looked at them and were glad you'd left your gun behind. The odds were better carrying a club into a rock-slide.

"Name?"

The clerk's tone wasn't entirely impolite. I told him and he lifted a flesh-colored receiver off a cradle behind the desk without dialing and waited and then repeated my name into the mouthpiece. After a second he replaced the receiver and nodded at the two men. Without actually touching me they steered me to the right and around a corner to the elevators. We stepped into an open car and when the doors were closed I stood for the frisk by the redhead while the shaven-headed one watched and then the redhead stepped back and his companion patted me down again. Finally he took off my hat and ran a finger around inside the sweatband.

"Do I get to do you now?" I asked when he returned it.

Neither of them said anything. A button got pushed and I had the quietest ride ever, watching the numbers light up in orange along the top of the car. It stopped on eight with a tiny sigh and the doors slid open on the biggest hotel room in the world.

They had removed all the partitions from that floor, including those defining the hallway, so that we stepped directly into a city-block of room carpeted in midnight blue with brushed-aluminum panels on the walls—the effect was of a room lined in dull silver—and track lighting in the suspended ceiling and a stately row of green-draped windows like the arches at Versailles. The office and the living area blended into each other in such a way that the tenant could rise in the morning from the rumpled king-size bed in the far left corner and go through the door at the rear for a shower in what was presumably the bathroom and put on one of the couple of dozen suits hanging in the walk-in closet with its doors folded open by the bed and take a leisurely breakfast at the table between two of the windows and then go to work at the big no-nonsense slab oak desk with a tufted leather swivel behind it inside an L of wooden file cabinets in the near right corner. The place had everything but a doghouse.

The dog that would have used it was sixty pounds of

short tawny coat stretched over broad muscled chest and a pair of haunches that stood out like fireplace fenders when it got up from its place in the center of the blue carpet to trot over and sniff at my ankles. It had a square head and skimpy ears and round black eyes set close above a cartoon muzzle that bent down. It didn't growl or bark. Pit bulls generally don't make much noise even when they're gnawing happily away on your tibia.

"Take the mutt out for a walk or something."

The speaker was tying his tie in front of one of the mirrored closet door panels, all tapered back and narrow hips in a tight vest and pinstriped brown pants. The red-head got a leash off the coffee table and snapped it onto the dog's collar and pulled it away from me, or tried to. It wanted to go on sniffing at me but he quirted it behind the left ear with the leather loop and it lost interest. It had a bobbed tail and when it turned to enter the elevator a ragged white scar rippled on its left shoulder. The hair had grown in around it in conflicting grains.

"Lose it in traffic if you can," said the man at the mirror. The elevator doors closed.

"Garibaldi's a good dog."

This was Tomaso Acardo, seated at the table between the windows in his shirtsleeves with a napkin tucked elegantly inside his collar. He was sawing away at a piece of roast chicken on a china dish. A tall-stemmed glass half filled with yellow wine stood at his right elbow.

"He's a mange. And a loser to boot."

"To win you must first care how the fight comes out. Are you a dog man, Mr. Walker?"

"Depends on the dog."

He sipped wine and removed the droplets from his moustache with a corner of the napkin. "I bought Garibaldi from a man who fought him in Iroquois Heights. The dog was recovering from a bad slashing and the man was making arrangements for his next fight. I paid him five hundred dollars over and above the veterinary bill. I can't stand to see a dumb brute suffer. Giovanni was keeping him for me."

"I guess a dog needs room to run," I said.

"It is large, isn't it? My brother believed in big."

"Al Capone shit." The other man reached a pinstriped brown jacket off a hanger in the closet and turned around. "The building's up for sale. Whoever buys it can raze it or make a monument out of it or turn it into a planter. I'm moving the operation up to Grosse Pointe where it belongs."

"Your father won't like it," said Tomaso.

"My father's dead. Fucking spicks hit him in the head and fed him to a crusher."

"We don't know that."

"Right. He makes an appointment to meet somebody in a beergarden at Joy and Evergreen, he don't say who, and the last anybody sees of him he's on his way there with a carnation in his lapel. He fell in love with a black barmaid and now they're raising kids and tulips in Mombasa."

"I didn't say he wasn't taken against his will."

Frank Acardo looked at me for the first time. He had dark brown hair combed over his ears, a long jaw, small eyes that snapped, and a hook nose that on his uncle would be called aquiline but that on him could have been used to open bottles. His face beveled back from it sharply like the hull of an icebreaker. He was my age and a whole lot more ugly.

"You," he said. "What's your connection with Sam Mozo?"

"He's my aunt."

"Fucking comedian. I've had a tail on that little Spanish asshole since September. He stops on West Grand River to jaw with you, one of my men follows you up to this crummy third-floor office afterwards. What's it say on the door? 'A. Walker Investigations.' I get to wondering what a private muzzle's got to talk about with Sam Mozo. I put Tomaso there on the muzzle's ass."

"Nice job," I told Tomaso. "I didn't spot you."

"I helped smuggle Allied fliers over the Alps into Switzerland under Mussolini's nose. You're a difficult man to keep in sight. I imagine it's your habit."

"Tomaso, he's got manners," Acardo continued. "Maybe an invite from him gets better results than Mozo got trying to coax you into that fucking Lincoln of his. Also why risk good talent on a dark horse when that's what family's for? What the fuck are you grinning at?"

"Only in Detroit," I said.

"What."

"There are terrorists running all over Europe in bedsheets killing people for looking American and there's enough fission piled up in each hemisphere to blow the world into marbles several times over. The sun is burning itself out and what the governor spends on hairdressers would feed a Third World country for a year. Only in Detroit would a cheap gangster bother to air his Jimmy Cagney impression for a private detective like it was 1931 and Eliot Ness was banging on his door."

Tomaso chuckled in that deep rumbling bass. Frank swung his hook on him. "Ain't you got a gravel pit to inspect or something?"

"You're overdoing the ain'ts and double negatives. Mr. Walker knows we send our young to college."

"*Zio Capro.*" The hook swung back my way. "After talking to Mozo you went straight from your office to police headquarters. Why?"

"I lost my virginity. I thought someone might have turned it in."

"Hey, I can make a call and find out what you were doing there."

I took a seat in an upright chair covered in yellow vinyl. It looked to be the most uncomfortable there and it probably was. I didn't want to be comfortable in the sort of room that would contain Frank Acardo. I broke a fresh cigarette out of the deck. I lit it and dragged over a smoking stand with some tea-colored butts in it and got rid of the match. I'd taken my second pull before he realized I wasn't going to answer him. He kept the lid on.

"Listen, I don't want to get ugly."

"Too late."

"I could bounce him a little." This was the guy with the clean head in hat and topcoat standing sentry at the elevator. He had a thin voice for what he was.

"It wouldn't work." Frank was studying me now with his hands in his pockets. "It's got to do with that dark meat Tomaso saw you hanging out with at the museum, don't it? He overheard some of it. Uncle Goat's got good ears; they're just about the only thing about him that's good. Okay, I can cut a deal same as my old man. What are your rates?"

"You couldn't afford them."

"Mr. Acardo." Baldy was pleading now.

"Save it, Jonesy. Look, it ain't like we don't want the same thing. Mozo killed my old man, he's out to put the hurt on your girlfriend for some reason. You guys don't like working for free, shit, who does? So maybe I make it a little more worth your time to help put him underground."

"What's wrong with Jonesy?"

"His hands are tied. Mine too." He leaned back on the arm of a big leather chair, hands still in his pockets to show how tightly they were tied. "See, I got people to answer to same as everyone else. My old man sat on the board of the national organization but me, I'm just one of the fish. I know Sam Mozo offed him, know it here"—he took out a hand and tapped his left lung—"but it's just like in court, I got to prove it. You put your nose to it, bring me something I can take to the board, the rest is up to Jonesy and Flynn there outside taking the mutt for a pee. Next day you get a brick in the mail, only it ain't no brick. Get yourself a decent office in a building with an elevator, hey, maybe even some blonde snatch sits out front telling people she's your secretary, how's that?"

"I've got a client."

"Okay, you like it black, I can get next to that. Scratch the blonde. You won't go to hell for taking money from two places for the same job. It gets done, everyone's happy. What do you say, sport?"

"Why don't you just call me chamaco?"

"Now, what the hell is that?"

"I have an idea you won't be able to meet Mr. Walker's price." Tomaso slid his knife and fork onto his plate and pushed it away to finish his wine.

"Not money, then," said Frank. "We're an old established firm, we got friends all over. Maybe we can do something for you."

"Maybe you can," I said.

16

Mary M said, "No."

It was daytime and she was wearing red slacks and pink high-top tennis shoes like the kids wear and a black cableknit sweater with a white collar rolled out over the neck. From the waist up it looked like a Catholic school uniform and she looked like a particularly precocious sixteen-year-old despite the lines in her face. She was looking at Jonesy, who had reached back into some memory and removed his hat from his shaved head on her doorstep.

"His bed and board will be taken care of," I said. "He's housebroken, they tell me. You won't even know he's here."

"You got that right. He won't be here."

"Inside or parked out front, he'll be here. I'd prefer inside. I'm sold that the man who's been threatening Iris has gotten to one of your tenants. The selling job was yours when you showed me how you handle unwanted guests. Inside, Jonesy will get the chance to stop something before it starts. It's better than no chance at all. Think of him as the house eunuch."

"Watch that shit," he said.

He hadn't spoken at all in my car on the way over, but that hadn't anything to do with his boss's instructions to cooperate instead of dribbling me. He'd watched the scenery with alert interested eyes, turning his head all around like a dog on its first automobile trip in a long time. He had to have been tired of the sights in the Adelaide. If you didn't know he had a gun strapped to his ribs under the topcoat you'd have wanted to scratch him behind the ears, if he had hair and a personality.

I wasn't getting around Mary M. The pixie impression was all in her bright eyes and small sharp features; behind that she was case steel. I said, "Why don't we put it to Iris? Let her decide."

"I know what she'll say."

"Let's hear it anyway."

She had on loose flowered lounging pajamas and the cork-soled shoes I had seen before. Jonesy appreciated her. His round flap ears moved back and his face smoothed out even further; much more and it would have been gone entirely. Iris gave him a quick glance and thanked Mary M, who had fetched her. It was a polite dismissal.

Mary M hesitated, then decided. "I'll be close." She went down the hall.

Jonesy said, "Heavy chick."

"Who's Kojak?" asked Iris.

I introduced them. "He doesn't need much care. A biscuit now and then, maybe some rawhide to chew on. He breaks necks for Frankie Acardo. Guys who break necks for a living are better than the average run at preventing necks from being broken."

"So that's why you went to see him."

"Partly. I was also curious like I said. I make deals. That flaming sword gets heavy."

"Thanks, I'll go with what I've got." But she didn't move.

"Mary M's got a big handicap when it comes to this kind of thing," I said. "She's got a heart. Jonesy, what do you do when somebody gets too close?"

"Kill 'em."

"See?"

"I had it to here with killers," she said. "They stink in bed and they're boring to listen to. What if somebody counts the doors wrong coming back from the bathroom at night, he going to blow a hole through them?"

"You're not worried about that. You just don't take to the idea of someone babysitting you. No one does, including babies. I can't do any kind of job looking for your father if I have to keep calling here every hour or so to ask if your throat's been cut yet. This isn't negotiable."

The corners of her nostrils lifted at that. I braced myself, but after a beat she said: "Well, where's he sleep?"

"Down, boy," I told Jonesy.

Driving away from there I felt like singing. Things couldn't have taken a better turn if an uncle had died and left me Uniroyal. Federal bodyguards miss details while they're studying their reflections in their custom nickel-plated pearl-handled pocket pistols, and policemen are always worrying about their wives and their hairlines. The worst any of them can pull if their protectees get splashed is a ninety-day suspension, or the boot if there are headlines involved. Shields like Jonesy treated their responsibilities more personally because if they fell down they stood a better than even chance of dying young; their employers didn't believe in severance pay. Besides, this one liked his work. So he was sitting on a chair outside Iris' room with his gun in his lap, happy as a mother snake protecting her young, and I was back in the traces.

I got Mr. Charm's notebook out of my pocket and went over his entries again while waiting for a light on St. Antoine. I'd been carrying it around since leaving his office and so far osmosis wasn't working. "212, S.M., $5,000" was still intriguing. The only S.M. I'd met in the case had opened a big door for me. I was hoping he would open at least one more. The driver behind me tooted and I turned on the green in the direction of Tireman.

It was half-past noon when I entered the motel lobby. I was counting on the towheaded clerk with the spiky moustache being on a break. I was right. In his place a black girl with glasses and the company red blazer smiled at me. She was barely tall enough to see over the desk.

I smiled back, trying to look tired. It didn't take much trying. "Single for the night. Two-twelve, if I can get it. I got the best sleep I ever had in a motel last time I stayed there."

"Four-oh-eight's quieter," she said. "It's an inside room."

"I'm claustrophobic."

She checked her card file. The room would be occupied. A vacancy would be too easy. I was flipping through my own brain index of alternate stories when she slid a registration blank in front of me.

"It's a corner room in back, second level. Just drive around behind the building and take the stairs. I guess you know that if you stayed there before."

I thanked her anyway and signed "L. P. Wimsey" above a phony address. I gave her thirty-five dollars and she gave me a brass key that lay in my pocket like a hand truck. I saw no sign of Lester Hamilton on my way around the building. No one was reading plate numbers in his place.

It was a room on an open hallway overlooking the parking lot, with a picture window in front so the tenant could sit on the baby sofa and watch his car being stripped. The sofa and chair were gray and so was the rug and the coverlet on the double bed. The dresser and writing table were glass-topped, the bathroom clean and small and unremarkable. The closet was a doorless alcove with a rod and half a dozen theft-proof hangers slotted into steel loops. On the wall over the bed hung a duck-hunting print in a pressed wood frame, bolted in place, its figures reversed in a mirror built into the partition opposite it, facing the bed.

I wondered about the mirror. I threw my hat on the bed, walked up to the glass, and leaned my forehead against it, blocking out light with my cupped hands. A pair of sad brown eyes stared back. The mirror was opaque, from this side anyway. I walked around the room a second time. I pulled the dresser away from the wall and looked behind it and felt along the baseboard. If necessary I'd have gotten down and groped around under the bed, a job I always saved for last because that was where ghosts bred and multiplied. I didn't have to. I found it socketed in the knob that screwed onto the bedside lamp and held the shade in place, a metal plug the size of a thumbnail, with a waffled top and wires running down inside the harp into the base of the lamp itself.

I had an idea where they would lead from there. I checked it out. I let myself out into the hall and around the corner to the linen closet I knew I'd find there. The door was locked, but linen doesn't rate a dead bolt. I slipped it in less than a minute using the edge of my ID.

The closet was four feet square, all bare drywall with an exposed bulb screwed into the ceiling and a chain switch hanging down. It was part of a crawlspace between the inner and outer rooms. The shelves had been removed — the holes where the brackets had been looked like puckered wounds — and someone had sawed a square out of one wall and installed a window. I saw the room I had just been in, turned backward as if I were looking in a mirror, which in fact I was, or rather through one. Two-way mirrors were hot stuff when I was a kid, but now everyone has one in his front door and nobody much thinks about them, least of all the guests in well-maintained motels. On a stand in front of the glass someone had erected a video camera with its lens looking into the room. With a toe I nudged its trailing wires where they disappeared through a hole in the floor. I knew where they came out. I found the catch on the camera and slid out the tray that held the tape. It wasn't holding anything but air.

There was nothing else to see. I wiped off everything I'd touched and smeared both doorknobs on my way out of Eldon Charm's private motion picture studio. I didn't reset the lock. No police seal meant I'd beat the cops there. I owed them a break.

Back in 212 I stretched out on the coverlet, smoking a cigarette and watching myself in the mirror. It gave me a crawling sensation, like looking at the smooth black surface of the water filling a mineshaft three hundred feet deep, and I knew then that I would never pass another mirror without feeling the clammy chill of blind white things swimming in and out through empty eye-sockets at the bottom.

There was no reason for that. Charm had supplemented his night-manager's income videotaping married executives and their secretaries nooning on the premises — probably in every room in the motel that bordered on a linen closet, if the other entries in his notebook meant anything — and selling them back to his subjects at four-digit rates. Chances were he had compromised Sam Mozo similarly, making himself enough of a nuisance to be removed, but in the heat following Jackie Acardo's disappearance only when it became convenient to remove him. Getting the list containing the license plate number of whatever flunky had planted the skull-and-crossbones in Iris' jewelry box would have been convenience enough. There was no reason to think the missing tape contained anything but the Latin butterball taking exercise with the wife of a city councilman, or maybe the city councilman himself, given the times. Or the mayor's cat.

No reason, except what was that to a loud little toad who

dressed out of the Warner Brothers wardrobe department and cut up expensive coats and custom leather seats and bragged about employing a Korean killer? Except for the fact that five thousand was at least twice as much as Charm was soaking any of the other initials in his notebook. Except for the fact that the beergarden where Jackie Acardo had agreed to meet someone just before he vanished was less than five minutes from where I was soiling the coverlet with my shoes and watching the gray spread through my hair in the mirror that was not a mirror. Except for the crawling sensation.

I didn't buy it for a second. The thing was too thorny with coincidence. It needed more work and the work wasn't going to get done while I was staring into that flooded mineshaft. I left the key for the maid to find and got out. If I was going to have nightmares about mirrors I'd have them in my home or my office where I could tell them to leave.

17

There is a new breed of detective abroad these days. It wears its suits tailored and never leaves the office except for two-hour lunches and to go home, doing all its gumshoeing on the telephone and at the computer console. It doesn't own a gun and it stokes up on chef's salads and Perrier and wouldn't be caught dead slipping a bellhop five dollars, although a year's lease on a late-model Jaguar for a congressional aide would not be beneath consideration. It doesn't even call itself a detective, preferring the term *consultant* along with whatever adjective is on the charts this season. But you can still find it in the Yellow Pages under "Private Investigators." Ma Bell knows.

In the office I called a firm I'd done business with before, that specializes in tracing the ownership of businesses and public corporations. That's all open record and theoretically you can get it from any county office for a minimal copying fee, but the labyrinth of subsidiaries and holding companies can delay the answers for weeks. (If you ever get the urge to scramble a computer, feed it the Catholic Church.) I reached a senior consultant finally and read off everything I could think of, including the motel on Tireman and the Park-a-Lot Garage and Sam Mozo and Man-

OFFICIALLY NOTED

uel Malviento, his real name. It was make-work and out-of-pocket, but I had dead-ended in room 212 and the thing wasn't tidy enough to hand to the police just yet. They would expect me to tidy it for them in twelve hours of interrogation. Even a doll like Mary Ann Thaler is still a cop, and anyway the Charm murder was Acting Lieutenant Leonard Hornet's. He'd book me as a material witness just to see bars on my face.

The senior consultant took it all down and offered to put the answers on my screen when he had them. I thanked him and said a private messenger would do. A grateful Japanese-American client had once suggested high-tech-ing my office at cost, but I'd opted for cash. The building's circuits wouldn't handle the load and besides, the equipment wouldn't go with the wallpaper.

Next I called Mary M's. Mary answered and I asked how Jonesy was getting on.

"Better than my refrigerator. Eight ham and cheese sandwiches so far, the last two without ham because we ran out. He's sublimating. Three of the girls propositioned him but he wasn't having any. What's he, gay? I *know* he's not a rabbi."

"He's a good bodyguard is what he is. Give him what he wants. Frankie A's good for it."

"Don't worry, I'm itemizing."

"How's Iris taking it?"

"He stands by the bathroom door while she's inside. How do you think?"

"Listen, this is no reflection on you."

"How isn't it? Just him sitting there says I can't look after my own guests. And you tell me one of them is some kind of a plant. Maybe this place wasn't paradise before you landed in it, but compared to where some of these girls came from it was next best. Do you have any idea what a man on the floor does to a house full of prostitutes trying to get straight? I'm fighting an epidemic of zipper fever here."

"I'm working on making him unnecessary."

"Work faster. You want to talk to Iris?"

"No, put Jonesy on."

"If he takes a bite out of the phone it goes on the bill."

I listened to house sounds for a minute. Then the receiver was lifted and I heard breathing. I asked Jonesy if Mary was still in the room.

"No. I got a door to stand in front of, pal."

"This'll just take a second. I want you to run a tab on these women who are hitting on you, especially the ones that don't give up. One of them's Mozo's. She'll be the most persistent."

"Gee, I never thought of that."

"I don't know you long enough to know how you think. When you find her, hold her. Don't kill her. She's the cops' link to that motel killing last night. If she ties it to Mozo we'll both have done our jobs. Maybe there's a bonus in it for you from Frankie."

"Yeah, like I get to keep my head."

There were any number of responses I could make to that, given his haircut, but I just told him good-bye. We were working together, sort of. There are courtesies.

The telephone rang as soon as I took my hand off it. It was Mary Ann Thaler, calling to say that ballistics had come up empty on the bullet I had dug out of Iris' front seat.

"That's okay," I said. "I think I know who put it there. Thanks again for running it. Turn anything yet on Charm?"

"Out of my hands." Her voice was cool and clean, like her office. "The robbery angle dried up. Safe could have been sprung anytime and he just didn't report it. I'm back to taxi holdups and liquor store heists."

"Before you got frozen out, did you find out if Charm had any kind of record?"

"As for instance blackmail?"

She got me with that one. I covered the pause with a cough. "I guess that's nothing new in hotel work."

"It's about as common as dentists who molest female patients. He had a fat bank account for a man who spent most of his time prowling hallways, but maybe he had a paper route. I wasn't with the case long enough to find out if we had a sheet on him. I could ask Hornet."

"Not that important."

"Somehow I didn't think it would be," she said. "You've got something that says blackmail?"

"Just a stab, so to speak. Murder's interesting."

"For you, maybe."

After lunch I had some traffic. A trim well-dressed woman in her forties with a bandage over one eye needed to find a witness to an accident. I ran the partial plate number she had through a contact in the Secretary of State's office, got three possibles, and charged her twenty dollars for ten minutes' work. I'd promised my contact lunch. Midwest Confidential called with some insurance work that could wait until next week and a woman in Cincinnati needed to find her ex-husband to sign some papers. I made some calls and tracked him down in East Detroit. That took me the rest of the afternoon. By the time I had the paperwork done it was dark out. I was starting to think about dinner when the telephone rang again.

"Mr. Walker?"

"Always has been."

"This is L. C. Candy, the trombone player?"

"Sure." I heard music on his end. I wondered if he was calling from the Kitchen.

"I wasn't sure I'd catch you before you went home."

"I never go home."

He said something else. Someone dropped a tray of glasses near him and I asked him to repeat it.

"I'm at a place called Captain Ted's Party in Ferndale."
He was shouting now. "It's on Woodward."

"Never heard of it."

"That puts you in the majority. Listen, you might want
to come up here."

"Why would I want to do that?"

"What?" The music was thumping louder. I told him I
was on my way. I had to say it twice.

The pavement was wet and slick with fresh snow bor-
dering it in ruled lines and pale headlamp beams and red
and green and amber traffic lights reflected on the surface
in a pastel wash. I drove past Captain Ted's Party the first
time and had to turn around and come back. It was a brick
building in a line of them with a small yellow electric sign
turned perpendicular to the avenue. It looked dark inside.
I parked in a tiny lot in back that was nowhere near full
and went in through the front door, set back in a tunnel.

There was no music now and the only light came from
a hollow square of rosy bulbs over the bar. I paused in the
entrance waiting for my pupils to dilate and one of the
pink-drenched figures seated at the bar straightened and
waved. I went over.

Candy took my hand in a firm grip and swept an olive-
drab jacket off the stool next to his, folding it in his lap. I
slid onto the stool. In that light he looked younger than
ever despite the untrimmed beard and out-of-fashion long
hair. His face was boyish, his turtleneck sweater too big
for him and turned back at the wrists.

The bartender, not much older, in a bowling shirt with
the collar open, was in front of me. I ordered a double
Scotch and started to ask Candy what was going on. At
that moment the light came on over the junior-size platform at the other end of the narrow room and he put his
finger to his lips. An old bald black man mounted the
platform carrying a trombone.

18

It started tentatively, with as much empty air coming out of the battered brass bell as music, but as he played on and his arm caught the rhythm of the slide it grew in confidence. What he'd lost in lung power he'd gained in maturity of phrasing, and if he would never have the driving originality of a leader he could still hold his own in a solo. The tune, what he gave us of it, was "Body and Soul." His playing lacked body. It had soul in bushels. At his age it had better, or else he had lived in vain.

It was wasted on most of the drinkers at the bar and in the thin line of booths across the narrow aisle. The name of the establishment was purely cosmetic. It wasn't a place to party, but to drink and not feel as if you were drinking alone. In time the bandstand would be replaced by another booth or a video game and the big old-fashioned neon juke standing next to it would be the only source of music. At that it would be more than the clientele deserved. The old man might have been plugged into the wall himself for all the attention he was drawing.

He had on an old black suitcoat that screamed Salvation Army on top of a green workshirt and distressed brown brogans poking out from under a rumpled pair of cuffs.

The bottom half of his face had fallen away and he had a white fringe hooked over his ears, the top of his head shedding haloes under the stingy spot. He didn't look anything like the brilliantined dandy with the thousand-candlepower smile in the picture Iris had given me. He looked like every old black man on Woodward. The trombone made the difference.

"Fleet Jackson — he's the bass, you know, in Domino — he's been telling me for a week I ought to come up here, check out this old dude that plays like me," Candy said, next to my ear. "I didn't think anything about it. He thinks all horn players sound the same. Well, tonight I got restless, it's my night off. I get here just as the guy's warming up, blowing a few licks. I didn't stop to ask who he is. I don't ask questions I know the answers to. I called you. Did I do right?"

He had some Coke in the bottom of a glass full of ice. I got the bartender's eye and pointed at the glass and paid him for a fresh Coke and my Scotch.

"Talk to him?"

"Don't think I didn't want to," Candy said. "He's been sitting back there in a corner booth all night sucking down beers. If he started to leave I'd of nailed him. That old man taught me everything I know about the 'bone and we never even met. I got a million questions to ask. But I figure the man working for his daughter gets first crack."

I shielded my wallet from the rest of the room with my body and got out two fifties and started to slide them across the bar toward him folded. He made a flicking-away gesture with his fingers.

"If you can get him to hang around a couple of minutes when you're through," he said.

I put the bills back. "I'll tie him down if that's what it takes."

George Favor had brought a glass of beer with him to

the platform. When he finished playing — Candy and I applauded, stirring boozily curious looks from the others at the bar — he drained it, lowering the glass twice between swallows, then set it back down on the platform and fiddled with his slide. He belched dramatically. Finally he lifted the horn again and started "I'm Getting Sentimental Over You," with some fifties-style jazz variations on Tommy Dorsey. Between licks he took the mouthpiece away from his lips and breathed.

When the bartender came by I asked him who the wheezer was. Polishing a glass he glanced over to see which wheezer that might be and shrugged. "Boss took him on when the group quit. He was the only one showed for the audition. I forget his name. Maybe I never heard it. They treat us like mushrooms here: keep us in the dark and throw shit on us."

"What's he get, scale?"

"What's scale?"

"Forget it."

" 'Gimme a Bud,' that's all he ever said to me. I think it's his pay. I got orders not to ring it up."

"He earns it, sounds like."

He shrugged again. "That stuff's okay. Heavy metal, that's my meat. I had a group."

"Who didn't?"

I watched Candy watching Favor. His eyes glittered, he was leaning forward on his stool with his hands on his thighs. I didn't have a handle on him yet. Maybe he would never be anything more than just a good musician because his hero was less than great. Or maybe he was hearing things I didn't and never would. Music is the great divider. We're all tied to the primal beats that celebrated victory and commemorated defeat when fire still belonged to the gods; beyond that it's anyone's call. Detroit has known the thumping of hollow logs by war clubs gripped in red hands and the military tattoo of British and French regiments and the four-four beat of jazz soaked in bootleg hootch, it's known Motown and country and disco, and half the population listened and said it was good and the other half wanted to be let alone to hear the rhythm of living and not living and the long bleak bridge between. The man on the platform would belong to the second half, but he was also the part of the half that made the music. He could be dead tomorrow and the thing that would separate him from all the other old men who would be dead tomorrow would be the instrument he was playing. He knew it. It was in the way he kept returning the mouthpiece to his lips after each barely successful attempt to fill his lungs, and it was in the way his knuckles turned yellow as he worked the slide. Maybe L. C. Candy knew it too, and maybe that's what he was hearing.

Our applause when Favor finished might have been for the clock behind the bar. The old man picked up his glass and stepped down gingerly from the platform and hobbled over to the bar and set the glass on top without once looking at us.

"Gimme a Bud."

The bartender shot me a glance that said, "See?," drew one, and set it in front of him, scooping up the empty mug with his other hand. Favor carried the fresh one and his instrument over to the corner booth in back and laid the trombone on one of the seats and lowered himself onto the other. I touched Candy's arm and took my Scotch over there.

"George Favor?"

He looked up at me with no interest in his expression. The whites of his eyes were cream-colored and prickles of sweat glinted in the deep folds on his forehead, although the room was not overly heated. He was breathing heavily. "You got a subpoeny?"

I shook my head. He went on looking at me, waiting, and I realized he hadn't seen it. I said, "No."

"Last time someone I didn't know come up on me in a bar he had a subpoeny. Said I seen the owner of my building fucking up the furnace. I told him go fuck yourself. He said they stick my ass in jail I didn't testify. I said I been in jail. Well, I didn't testify and they didn't stick my ass in no jail. Man settled up. I didn't get nothing, though. I already moved out."

"My name's Amos Walker. I'm a private investigator. I've been looking for you for two days. You leave a crooked trail."

"You do one-nighters two hundred times a year when you're young you get used to traveling light. You sure you ain't got a subpoeny?"

"Why, did you see something again?"

"Son, I didn't see that whitey fucking up the furnace and he was as close to me as you are. Eyes, shit. You don't need to see to play music. Unless you in the symphony." He said *sim-phoney*. I asked if I could sit down.

"They your legs, how should I know? Just don't sit on the livelihood."

Setting down my glass I lifted the trombone gently and laid it on the table along the brick wall. The metal was cool and smelled faintly of oil. The booth was a tight fit. There was one more of them than the place could handle, and six more than it needed. I asked him what he'd been in jail for. His fallen-away face twisted wryly. "Well, now, what you think?"

I nodded, just for me. He wouldn't see it. "Still smoking?"

"No, I gave that shit up. Emphysema."

"Sweet Joe still is. He's entitled. He's dying."

"Big deal."

"You don't like him?"

"I never knowed him enough to like or don't like. We just played together for a little while. What I mean by 'big deal,' I know a lot more people that died than didn't. It must not be too hard. I thought he was dead already."

That one was wearing thin. I said, "He saw you when you were working at the pancake place four years ago. You talked. That's how I knew you were sitting in at the Kitchen, only Drago Zelinka didn't know where you went from there."

"Z, that hunky prick. Union had him scared shitless. He could of hired me on, stop all that strike talk, why'd he think I was coming down there all the time, I love to play? A job, that's all it ever was. I buried every friend I had that lived to make music. They all starved or drunk their-selves under the ground before they was forty. Playing or washing dishes, it's all the same to me so long as I eat. And get something to wash it down." He toasted me with his mug and drank.

"I saw you up there just now. It isn't just to eat and swill beer."

"Say you're a cop?"

"Private. My client's looking for her father."

"She older than twelve?"

"And then some."

"What the hell's she at looking for him, then? Nobody needs Daddy after twelve. I was thirteen when I split. Crazy old cotton-picker, he take his hat off when the Man come around, say sir and mister like he never heard of Lincoln. You know who taught me to play tailgate? Old fart in a Atlanta whorehouse. I learned the scales and caught my first dose of clap the same night. Daddies, they don't teach you nothing you need to know in the real world."

"He the one gave you the horn?"

"My old man, you kidding? He didn't know eight bars from a shit-beetle."

"The guy in the whorehouse."

"Oh, him. Hell, no, I cut that line when he tried to bugger me right there in the parlor. I got this one for ten bucks in a junk shop downtown. Hocked the best 'bone I ever had, fine silver-plated thing had a tone like a Rolls Royce horn. They sold it out from under me. Didn't think I'd ever scratch together the dough to redeem it. Son, I been up and down and all around the block. They tell you that's what makes 'em great in this gig. Don't you believe them. If you wasn't born that way all the empty-belly nights in the world won't make you that way. I wasn't. *They* know it." He inclined his head in the direction of the silent drinkers at the bar. "You think they wouldn't pay attention if I was any better than just good?"

I sipped from my glass. As a philosopher I was about three drinks behind him. "This father my client wants to find," I said. "She says it's you."

"Tell her I'm broke."

"She doesn't want money."

"She's no daughter of mine, then. I'll take as much as I can get."

"Your name is on her birth certificate. She was born in Jamaica. Conceived there too, probably. You were playing the Piano Stool in Kingston with your band."

"I never been in Jamaica."

I fished out the snapshot Iris had given me of her parents and put it in front of him. After a second he picked it up and held it very close to his eyes. He got up, using the table for leverage, and hobbled over to the jukebox, studying it in the pink and green neon. The bartender had turned off the overhead spot and stuck a quarter in the machine. A slow rock instrumental was playing that sounded like an expressway pileup in slow motion. After a long time Favor came back to the booth. He was smiling. Store teeth gleamed dully in the poor light. He plunked himself down and slid the snapshot across to me. I put it back in my pocket.

"Fine-looking woman," he said. "Daughter look anything like her?"

"Even better."

"They come prettier every year. That's how you know you're getting old."

"Recognize the mother?"

He wasn't listening. "This lady I knowed hit me with a paternity once. Nineteen fifty-eight it was. She give it up finally."

"This one isn't after money; I said that. She just wants to meet her father."

"This lady I'm talking about give it up on account of a lab test I took. Son, you can sterilize a scalpel in my jizzum. I was to have a kid, you can call me Joseph. That's what it'd take."

"You're sterile?"

"You might drop your voice some. I had me a reputation in this town at one time. Maybe I still do. I ain't got it up since Nixon and the memory means something."

I turned my glass inside its ring. "If you'd told Glen Dexter that, maybe you wouldn't have broken up."

"What do you hear from Glen?" He choked off a coughing fit to ask the question.

"Nothing. She's dead. She tried having a baby too late and it killed her. A long time ago. I talked to her niece."

He filled his cheeks from the mug and swallowed. He closed his eyes. I couldn't tell if he was remembering or waiting for the matter in his lungs to settle. He opened them finally.

"Back then you didn't just up and tell a woman you wasn't as much man as she thought," he said. "I didn't make mistakes I wouldn't be playing this dump."

135

"Your story can be checked."

He was a moment coming back to it. "St. John's. Those places never throw away their records. We go down together you want. Personally I'd just as soon take the credit, but like I said, Jamaica, I never been."

"What about the picture?"

The rock tune ended. He patted my hand. His was small, like the rest of him, and calloused like Candy's where he gripped the slide.

"I got to start playing before our friend at the bar gets grateful for the dead again. Tell the lady music's crazy. One note looks pretty much like all the others on the sheet till you push it through the right instrument."

He picked up the trombone and his beer and left me. The light came on over the platform and he got all the way through the first chorus of "Night Train" before I stirred. I finished my drink and got up and leaned down next to L. C. Candy at the bar, resting a hand on his shoulder. "He's yours."

"Great," he said. "I don't know what to ask him first."

"Doesn't matter. He won't give you any straight answers."

19

The trouble was, I believed him.

An old man with no money and nothing to hang on to but a bottomless beer mug and a ten-dollar horn had no reason to lie about a thirty-year-old affair. And if you accepted that, then every step I had taken so far, beginning with the first, had led in the wrong direction. Driving back to Detroit, through blocks of houses with snow-frosted roofs and Neighborhood Watch decals like an Orwellian Disneyland, I was surrounded by the emptiness of sound detective work gone to sawdust. It was a premature orgasm of a case, a quest for a silver chalice that turned out to have MADE IN TAIWAN stamped across its bottom. Turn in your portable fingerprint kit, Walker. As a sleuth you're a joke. Forget about being born great; mediocrity is past your reach. If you laid all of history's bonehead moves end to end beginning with Moses turning toward the desert and away from the Arabian oilfields, you had a fair approximation of Amos Walker's career as a hawkshaw. He wasn't fit to shine the shoes on Bulldog Drummond's flat feet.

It starts out bad, one scrap of wrong information, and gets worse, like a part cast from an imperfect die and then another die made from that part and so on, each part less accurate than the last. Iris had got some bum dope from the Piano Stool's half-senile former owner and I'd grabbed it and run with it. I'd found the man I was looking for, only to learn I'd been looking for the wrong man. There is no success as complete as a systematic failure.

This was too big not to share. I got off the Chrysler and turned down St. Antoine, accelerating to beat a county salt truck getting set to make the swing from East Ferry, and parked in front of Mary M's. The bell was answered by a woman I didn't know, a tall order with brittle blonde hair blown into a lethal ridge across her forehead and a spoon-shaped face with tiny eyes and bee-stung lips and a nose that had had some work done on it so that it looked like a button in the middle of her face. She had on an orange-flowered housecoat cinched at the waist with a red plastic belt and she smelled of the kind of perfume that cost about as much as gasoline and made a similar statement. She was breathing hard.

"EMS?" she demanded.

I shook my head. Something cold climbed my belly.

"Jesus Christ, it's twenty minutes since I called nine-eleven."

"Called them for what?"

"I mean, I got better service from Byron, and he broke my fingers once when I held back on him."

I got the lapels of the housecoat in my hands. "Called them for what?"

"See for yourself. Jesus Christ. I'm going to look like shit in the morning I don't get my ten hours."

I let go of her and powered past. A lamp burned in the entryway, its shade on crooked, and the hallway stretched dark beyond it to where some people stood in the light spilling out of an open door at the end. I pushed a path through the women in dresses and slacks and nightgowns and less and almost tripped over Jonesy lying on the floor with his legs in the hallway. Someone had shoved a pillow under his bald head and Mary M, dressed in the same red slacks and black sweater I'd seen her in last, knelt next to him dabbing with a wet washcloth at the blood on his fore-head. Something had opened a deep gash from his right temple to the crease between his brows. His eyes were half open with the glaze of shock over them.

"Where's Iris?"

Mary looked up at me. She had trouble focusing. "She's gone. They took her."

"Who's they?"

"Nobody saw them. I was upstairs, the girls were all in their rooms. They must have broken in and hit him and grabbed her and left. Some bodyguard."

"You told me you didn't need one. Anybody hear any-thing?" I spotted platinum-haired Sara in the group.

"A car taking off," she said. "Big engine."

The room was a bedroom, in good order with the bed made and a magazine lying open on the arm of a chair covered in green chintz. *Working Woman*, if it matters. The closet door was open and I recognized a couple of the outfits hanging inside. "This room is Iris'?"

Mary said it was. She was pressing the washcloth to Jonesy's wound, trying to stop the bleeding. "I think they cracked his skull."

I squatted and groped inside his jacket. My fingers touched the alligator butt of an automatic in an underarm holster. He hadn't drawn it. I gestured at Mary, who took her hand away. I peeled aside the wet cloth. The gash was a long inverted comma with the point on top; an upward blow. I had seen others like it, in martial arts training in the army when someone miscalculated. "He say anything?"

"He was out cold when I found him," Mary said. "That's been half an hour anyway. Where the hell is that ambu-lance?"

A telephone rang. I thought at first it was the siren. She glanced toward the hallway and I stepped out over Jonesy and unhooked the receiver from the wall.

"Hey, chamaco."

"Your boy Ang's getting sloppy," I told the accent. "He left him alive."

Mozo hesitated. "Off a man, anybody can do that. You got to be good to just put heem down. Hey, you didn' tell me you was working with them Acardos."

"Get to it."

"Hokay, hombre, you like to talk turkey. I can get next to it. You give me the tape, I don' cut off your girlfriend's head and send it to you parcel post, how's that?"

"What tape?"

"Man, you disappoint me. Just when I was starting to make you some respect. Time I met you, I didn' know you been in that Anglo's office, got the tape out of his safe. Hokay, this is America, land of opportunity, man got ambition, I don' hold it against him. Talking's over, chamaco. We trade."

"What, a tape for a corpse?"

A hand covered the mouthpiece on his end. Through my other ear I heard the siren now, switching from wail to yelp as it came off the Chrysler.

"Amos?" It was Iris.

"You all right?"

"My ass is freezing, what do you think? All I've got on is pajamas and a coat."

She started to say something else. The receiver was taken away.

"The tape, chamaco. Or the rest of her gets as cold as her ass. Call you later, your office."

"Just a second."

"Thirty minutes. You don' answer, I mail a package." The connection broke.

The ambulance was on the street now. I turned my back to the racket and called Information and got the number of the Adelaide Hotel. After a moment the clerk in the lobby put me through to Frank Acardo.

When I finished talking the attendants were in the hall-way, sporting the snappy dark blue police-type uniforms they wear now and carrying a stretcher. I tried to get Mary M's attention but she was too busy herding her houseguests out of the way. Heading out I checked the lock on the front door. Detective work, it never ends.

Flynn, the big red-headed Irishman who walked Tomaso Acardo's dog, was waiting for me in front of the Adelaide when I stood on the brakes. He opened the door on the passenger's side and got in. His hat perched warily on his big head with the narrow brim resting on the end of his pug. If there was still humor in his eyes it was lost in shadow.

I took off while he was pulling the door shut. He gripped the dash as we cornered. "How's Jonesy?"

"Still breathing when I left. You carrying?"

He bared his teeth at the windshield and said nothing. His big-jawed profile looked like flecked stone under the street lamps.

"Could be we're in a hell of a hurry just to wait," I said. "But if Mozo knows anything about kidnaping, when he calls he'll give me just enough time to get to the next contact spot and I can use the muscle."

"Just don't pick up any cruisers."

"I thought you mob guys owned the law."

"You read too many books."

It was quiet in the car for the next two blocks. I said, "Your boss gave you up without a fight. He always that generous with the talent?"

"Only when it involves Sam Mozo."

"You don't sound excited."

"They ought to make all the little hard-ass punks wear numbers so we can tell them apart."

"Your boss's old man was one. Back in the dry time." I spun onto Grand River, spraying slush. He leaned on the door handle.

"Prohibition. The good old days. I had it to here with that crap. The Purple Gang, me and Jonesy could take the whole bunch apart with our hands. Tight-ass little Jews, sharp suits and tommy guns. Christ."

"You two friends?"

He shut down. "I just work with him."

"I didn't hit him."

"All I know is you don't just walk up to Jonesy and take him while he's looking at you. Not if he don't know you."

"I was thinking the same thing."

There wasn't any more time to talk. I parked in a tow-away zone in front of my building and the telephone was ringing when we reached the outer office. The lock was stubborn at first. I took a deep breath and tried the key again. The tumblers let go and I speared the receiver on the dive.

"Chamaco, I was about to hang up."

I made an effort not to sound out of breath. "Your watch is fast."

"No way. Fi'teen t'ousan' dollars, accurate to within two seconds a month for a year. You got the tape?"

"No."

Pause. I heard echoes where he was. It sounded like a bus station.

"Lady's going to be disappointed, hombre. She could lose her head over a thing like that."

"You know I don't have it here or you'd have broken in and searched the place. I can get it, but it has to wait for morning."

"Why morning?"

"That's when the place opens where I've got it stashed. Eight o'clock."

"No jokes. My English ain' so good, I don' get them. Frustrates me. I lose my sense of humor."

"Straight dope."

" 'S'the only kind I deal." More echoes. "Hokay, chamaco, call you tomorrow. Eight-thirty."

We hung up. I looked at Flynn standing in front of the door. "I bought us some time."

"What's he want?"

"I figure it's a videotape made by a dead man named Charm at a motel Mozo owns on Tireman. Charm's retirement plan was wrapped up in hidden cameras all over the place."

"Blackmail?"

"Of Mozo, by Charm. If I read the dead man's notebook right, Mozo was the S.M. who was paying Charm $5,000, probably on a regular basis, for something Charm taped in room 212."

"Sex?"

"Mozo doesn't strike me as the inhibited type."

"A dope deal then," Flynn said. "Or a hit."

"Who's he hit lately?"

His Irish face ignited slowly. "Jesus. Not Jackie Acardo."

"It's a thin hunch. But you can spit from where Jackie was last seen to the motel."

"Jesus. You got the tape?"

"No. If I had I wouldn't need Mozo to answer my questions."

He touched his big jaw. Moonlight coming in through the Venetian blinds behind the desk striped him. "You play it right on the edge, don't you?"

"It's starting to feel like home." I switched on the desk lamp and opened the top drawer. I took out my Smith &

Wesson, checked the cylinder, and holstered the gun. He watched me clip the holster to my belt under my overcoat. "Where you going?"

"I think I know where he is."

"Mozo?"

"No, Jimmy Hoffa. Sure Mozo. I've got good ears. It's just what's between them that hasn't been working so hot." I picked up my keys. "You coming?"

"What if he's there and the girl ain't?"

"What if I meet him tomorrow morning and I don't have the tape?"

"Okay."

"Okay what?"

"Okay, I'm coming. Jesus. You dicks got to have everything spelled out."

We went downstairs. The city hadn't towed my Chevy, which was the first break I'd had in days.

2⊙

There was a three-quarter moon that night. The sky had cleared so that the snow held the light and made the street lamps look like bureaucratic meddling. The air was raw cold, as it always is at night in February when there is nothing between the city and the frozen core of outer space. When I got out on Griswold and closed the car door the handle stuck to my hand and needles of ice pricked my nostrils. Flynn turned up his collar and cursed a cloud of thick vapor. His topcoat was too light, but he wouldn't have chosen a heavier one. He was a man who liked to move. He looked heavy and slow; he wasn't. Coming around the front of the car he was like a snow tiger rolling the stiffness out of its muscles, becoming fluid as he came. There was evil beauty in that gait. It was too bad he was a gangster.

The Park-a-Lot Garage had a spectral quality in that light, gray seamless columns rising like Grecian pillars and dark metal gleaming softly where the cars were parked in tiers. The attendant's booth, visible from the street, was black and empty. The building looked deserted and we had been standing there almost five minutes before I picked out the faint yellow glow on the second level from the lights of the city itself behind the concrete latticework. I pointed at it and we entered at ground level.

The air inside seemed colder. It was rank with gasoline and sweet with auto exhaust. We found the painted fire door in the southeast corner and I pulled it open. A hinge squeaked, the sound sharp and echoing as in an amphitheater. We froze, but no one came to investigate. I picked up a square chunk of rough concrete that was used to prop open the door during the day and put it to work. I gestured to Flynn and he nodded and drew a black automatic from under his coat and took a stance at the base of the stairs while I climbed up. I unholstered the Smith & Wesson.

Stagnation lay like dead fish in that stairwell, remembering old urine and carnal nights, moonlight sliding down the color of pale flesh and folding soddenly over the steps. My breath curled around me. I held it.

The door at the top was open. I could see the office now, a glassed-in cubicle at the far end of the aisle I was standing in. Yellow light fanned out and painted streaks along the chrome bumpers of the cars parked in silent rows on either side. A shadow moved in the light.

I fished a penny out of my pocket and flipped it down the stairwell, arcing it out to miss the steps. It tinkled at the bottom like glass breaking. After a long time the air stirred in the shaft. Flynn was coming up, as quietly as smoke rising. When he was beside me, big and Irish and smelling faintly of Old Spice, I made a movement with the revolver to hold him there and worked my way down the aisle, scalloping around the ends of the diagonally parked cars. Traffic thundered along the John Lodge outside. It was a remote sound, a meteor shower in a different galaxy.

At the end of fifty feet I looked through the window from the shadow of a concrete post. Sam Mozo was sitting with his back to me, at a black pebbled-steel desk with three spindled stacks of white and yellow and pink papers on top, a different color to each spindle. He was smoking a brown cigarette and he had an old greasy radio on the desk tuned in to a Spanish-language station, so low I could barely hear it through the glass. I knew him by the roll of fat at the back of his neck and by his big white hat hanging on a corner of the radio. I smelled marijuana.

There was an old sprung sofa in the corner opposite the desk and Iris was lying on it, on her back with an arm flung across her eyes to block out the light. She was wearing the bright floral-print pajamas from that afternoon and she had her shoes off. While I was watching she turned over onto her right shoulder, showing her back to the office and Mozo. A jet of smoke left him in a silent sigh. I didn't blame him. It was a nice back.

From my angle I couldn't see if anyone else was in the office. In a building that depended on automobile space there wouldn't be much more to it. I wondered where Felipe was. More than that I wondered where Ang was.

He told me. Something scraped the floor, three times very fast like a dance step, and he came at me across the aisle from between two cars on that side, flying, a bent javelin in a tan suit, with his right leg knifed out in front and his trunk in line with it and his left leg steering his flight. Flynn fired, the automatic's report a ringing bark, but the bullet twanged off a post and punched a hole in a windshield. The Korean was still flying, coming down now, a lethal foot aimed at my throat and behind it the ugly ivory face scrunched into a toothy grin. My own snap shot missed and I threw myself back between a red Fiero and a four-wheel-drive truck and grasped the truck's door handle. It wasn't locked and I swung it open, bracing it with my body just as he piled into it. Glass sprayed. I fell back hard against the concrete wall and sat down. My wind was gone and so was my gun.

Coming up on my knees I groped for it. Ang was flopping like a trout, snarling something in what I assumed was Korean and trying to free his leg from the broken window in the truck's door. He had found his leverage and was starting to pull it out when my hand closed on the gun underneath the Fiero. I pitched forward, getting my feet under me, and brought the butt down hard on his cropped head. It made a sickening sound and he went limp. His foot hung up in the ragged hole in the glass. He dangled there.

I was sluggish. My lungs were filling slowly and my eyes stung. I wiped them with the back of the hand holding the gun. It came away bloody. I stumbled out into the aisle.

"Heads up!"

It was Flynn's voice. Instinctively I pivoted in the direction of the office, but there was nobody inside now. At that instant the world went up in white flame and two square headlamps came down the aisle at me with a roar. I dived back between the vehicles just as the big gray Lincoln swept past with Felipe at the wheel. The slipstream almost took me off my feet. I caught my balance and turned and saw Flynn standing spread-eagled in the glare of the headlamps at the end of the aisle, both hands stretched out in front of him clasping the automatic. He fired. The copper-jacketed bullet glanced off the windshield with a thin scream. Then the car struck him and he went up in the air, heels over head, his gun spinning away. He missed the ceiling, hanging just under it for an impossible length of time, then came back down in front of the Lincoln as it swung around the line of parked cars. It bumped over him twice and kept going into the turn. I sent two shots after it, but I was afraid of hitting Iris. I shattered a taillight. Then the car was gone. Tires yelped as it spiraled down to ground level and then out onto Griswold.

I heard sirens. I lurched down the aisle to where Flynn lay. His hat had come to rest upright nearby, untouched, display perfect. It wouldn't fit him now. I stood there with my lungs aching, trying to breathe. I thought of George Favor struggling with emphysema. A trickle of blood from my forehead reached my lips then.

It was that salt-and-iron taste that did it. I heard my gun clatter on the concrete, and that was the last thing I heard for a while.

An angel brought me to.

She had light brown hair that could have been honey blonde with no trouble, worn in bangs under a red plastic hairband, and baby blue eyes that were nowhere near the size of hen's eggs. The tortoiseshell glasses disappointed me a little. I had angels figured for twenty-twenty vision.

The walls of the place I was in were sea-green and so was the ceiling. I was in a bed with a sheet and a thin blanket drawn up under my chin and my head propped up on a foam-rubber pillow as thick as a book jacket. There was a steel rail on either side of the bed. That disappointed me a lot. Heaven looked a lot like a hospital room.

The angel had a message for me. "Boy, is your head going to hurt."

I dredged a hand out from under the covers and touched three or four yards of gauze folded and taped on my forehead. "Feels numb." I whispered it. There wasn't any moisture left in my mouth.

"That's the local. They dug out enough glass to rebuild the Crystal Palace and took sixteen stitches. Here." She put a blue plastic glass to my lips. I drank from it noisily and pulled a face.

"I didn't think they'd have to chlorinate the water in heaven."

"You're in Receiving. They're kicking you out of here as soon as you can stand up. Someone told them you don't have insurance."

149

It was starting to come back, in little bright sharp pieces, like flying glass. I put Lieutenant Thaler back in mortal perspective. "Flynn?"

"If you mean your buddy, they tagged him DOA. Dead on arrival at the floor is more like it; every bone in his body was broken. Hornet wants to nail you with felony homicide. It's why I came in his place. In his state they wouldn't let him in the door."

"He wouldn't fit through the door. What about the Korean?"

"Concussion and torn tendons. He'll be here a little longer. You want to tell me how he came to be in that condition? Otherwise I bust you for trespassing and assault."

"He won't press charges."

"He won't have to. We've got a dead man like I said." She waited. She was sitting in a lavender chair with her legs crossed in flesh-colored knit slacks, low-heeled brown boots on her feet with buckles on them.

"What time is it?" The vertical blinds were drawn over the windows and I couldn't tell if it was still dark out.

"Four A.M. My shift ended two hours ago. But I've been pulling doubles so long I wouldn't know what to do with time of my own."

I winched myself up on one elbow. I had on one of those Kleenexes they throw at your modesty in hospitals. I found the handle on the drawer of the nightstand and pulled it open. My cigarettes weren't inside. "I don't suppose you smoke," I said.

"No one does here. It's like Utopia." She was still waiting.

I doubled the pillow in the small of my back. "Sam Mozo snatched my client. We were trying to get her out."

"We?"

"Flynn, that's the only name I knew him by. He worked for Frank Acardo."

"Generous of Frankie."

———

150

"He likes Mozo less than the cops. You're the one told me that. I got just close enough to see they were holding my client in the garage when Ang jumped me. That's Mozo's pet Korean, the one with the bump on his head. By the time I was finished with him the Colombian got the woman into his car and his driver tried to make a road kill out of me. Flynn saved my hide by yelling. It didn't do him any good. Your team missed Mozo by five minutes."

"It wouldn't have if you'd called us."

"I had this crazy idea that riot guns and bull horns wouldn't be too healthy for my client."

"You think she's any healthier this way?"

"Maybe it was the wrong call," I said. "Maybe there wasn't a right one."

She touched her glasses. "This have anything to do with an Acardo soldier Emergency Medical Services scraped out of a house on St. Antoine tonight named Albert Jones?"

"That'd be Jonesy. He was guarding her when they took her. How is he?"

"They've got him upstairs too, with a fractured skull. He should make it. You go through Acardo men like I go through cotton balls." She paused. "You going to tell me who your client is and what Mozo wants with her?"

"Probably not."

"I didn't think so."

"Don't get your glasses in an uproar, Lieutenant. After last night she has a one-in-fifty chance of still being alive. Bringing the cops in would take it down to zero."

She didn't say anything for a minute. The morphine or whatever they had given me was keeping me drowsy. I was starting to float off on a warm cloud when she spoke. "You know who owns the motel where Charm was killed?"

"Someone named Gordenier."

"Where'd you get that?" Her voice was sharp.

I came awake. "I looked it up," I lied. I thought of Lester

Hamilton telling me about the A. G. that Charm had a noon appointment with on the day he was stabbed. "I got curious. I told you murder is interesting."

"Andrew Gordenier is a retired realtor. He fronts for Sam Mozo. Mozo owns the motel. Have you got anything to say about that?"

"No." I had to think for a long time before I said it. It was like swimming upstream in Jell-O. "I'm going to go night-night now, Lieutenant. Kick me if I snore." I closed my eyes.

I heard her get up after a minute. Behind my lids I was fighting to stay awake. I must have lost, because I never heard her leave. When I opened my eyes again, light was edging in between the window blinds.

The catch on the bedrail was a week coming undone. Finally I swung it down and rested a while before moving again. Getting up was like leaving the womb. The thin blue carpet was cool under my feet.

I found my clothes in a tin cabinet painted lavender to match the chair and put them on. I wondered if hospital decorators ever touched ground. The clothes were dirty from lying on the gritty oily floor of the garage, but my cigarettes were in my shirt pocket. I smoked one to gas the dope out of my veins and tied my shoelaces as tightly as I could on the theory that they would force blood to my head and I put on my hat and coat and walked out of there. The shoelace gimmick worked too well; my head was starting to throb.

There was no uniform at the door to the room. Mary Ann Thaler's brain didn't work in that straight a line. I was counting on that. The sun was coming up red in a cold sky through a window at the end of the deserted corridor. I found the elevator and pushed the button for the lobby.

The gray-haired floor nurse was on the telephone when I walked past the station. She didn't call out after me. I used the telephone in the waiting room near the entrance to order a taxi. I was told one was in the neighborhood and would be there in a couple of minutes. I shared the room with a man reading a magazine on the sofa. Visiting hours didn't start for another hour.

The cab pulled up in front of the glass doors and I went out. As I pushed open the door, in the glass I saw the man on the sofa put down his magazine and raise a hand to his mouth. His partner was on the taxi's rear bumper in a blue Plymouth before we left the parking lot.

21

I had a ticket for leaving my car parked on Griswold during snow-removal hours. It could have been worse. If there'd been a storm it would have been towed. I put the ticket in my pocket and got in behind the wheel. Rigor mortis had taken claim of the upholstery.

The blue Plymouth had pulled in behind a station wagon at the curb while I was paying off the cab driver. Its pipe was smoking in the morning chill. The Chevy's engine cut in with a touch of the key. I let it warm up for a minute, then put it in drive and swung into a U-turn. Halfway through I kicked it and shot through the entrance across the ground floor of the Park-a-Lot Garage.

The beefy attendant was just scrambling out of the booth when I exited on the Shelby side. The unmarked police unit, following, stood on its nose to avoid hitting him. I took off hard. I had two blocks on the Plymouth before it got shut of the building. After that we lost touch. I hoped for his sake the driver would answer to Mary Ann Thaler and not Acting Lieutenant Hornet.

Alderdyce hadn't closed his garage door. The snow had drifted in and formed quays around the foreign compact's rear tires and the jumble on both sides. When he didn't answer the bell I tried the knob. The front door wasn't locked. I passed through stale, shut-up air into the living room, where he was sitting slumped in the padded scoop chair in the same cardigan and jeans I had seen him in two days earlier. He hadn't had them off. His socks were dirty. His mouth was open and loud noises were coming out. It looked like the same bottle of Miller in his hand. It wasn't. Several generations of empties were lined up on the coffee table and on the floor around the base of the chair. One of the orphans had rolled and come to rest against the butt of the deer rifle in the corner.

"John." I shook him by the shoulder. He stopped snoring, smacked his lips, shifted his position, and didn't wake up. I caught the bottle before it toppled to the floor. It was half-full. I took a sip — the beer was flat — and stood it next to the others on the coffee table.

The television was on. A hard-looking brunette in her late forties, dressed in a leotard and shaggy knee-high socks without feet, was trying to tie herself into a bow on a padded studio floor with her ankles gripped in both hands. I figured she was accepting kickbacks from the American Chiropractic Association. I turned it off and lit a cigarette. I blew a lungful of smoke into John's open mouth.

He came awake rolling his eyes and coughing and turned in the chair and retched. There was nothing to bring up. He turned back and saw me and his confusion slid away. Pure hate took its place.

"You son of a bitch."

"I left my smelling salts at home. You all right?"

"I will be."

His tone was urgent. He clawed his way to his feet, almost fell back down, and wobbled out of the room, caroming off a wall. Water trickled in the bathroom. After a long time he came back and dropped into the chair. Relief and contentment softened his dark savage face. He looked around.

I picked up the half-full bottle and held it out. "Carbonation's gone."

He took it anyway and drained it at a gulp. Then he put his head back and closed his eyes. "I thought you left."

"Five six-packs ago."

"Time flies."

"I need your help."

He said nothing. He was either listening or asleep.

"A little hood named Sam Mozo is holding a woman," I said. "In a little while, if he hasn't killed her already, he's going to call me at my office to arrange a trade, the woman for some murder evidence I don't have. I can't go to the cops. If they find out she's a witness against him they'll slap her in protective custody, only there isn't any where the Colombians are concerned. She'll fall out of a hotel window or slip in the shower at County and break her neck. The Acardos want Mozo bad but I can't go to them because I've already cost them two men and Frank's the kind to teach me a lesson by letting Mozo burn the woman before he steps in. I have to have back-up at this meet. Mozo let his guard down last night but he won't today, and the trade won't be clean. Not after last night."

John's eyes were still closed. I was starting to think I'd lost him.

"I'm a cop," he said.

"A suspended one, who isn't feeling a lot of loyalty to the department just now. Also a good one."

"Hold the bullshit. What do you need?"

"If Mozo does call he won't let me pick the spot. I need you in your car in front of my building. It's a tail job."

"Can't do it. I'm ripped."

"I need you, John."

"*Don't* need me!"

He was wide awake now, his face savage again. "Every-where I look there's someone else needing me. My wife, my kids, the fucking department. Why the hell do you think I dropped out? I'm drowning, man."

I waited until he subsided. It didn't take long. His chest was working as if he'd just tried lifting something heavy and given up. My cigarette was singeing my fingers. I put it out.

"I don't have time to play psychiatrist," I said. "He could be trying to call right now. If I had my service transfer him here he'd get hinky. You're going to have to do your own pulling together. I hope you make it."

"Don't count on me, I told you."

"I hope you're there."

His eyes were closed again when I looked back at him from the door. The sight put ice in my belly. It was as if I'd never been there.

It was a bright cold day, the snow unbearably white under the sun. I wore dark glasses on the way to my building. My eyes felt swollen and heavy behind them and I could feel each of the sixteen stitches in my forehead, like embedded sparks. My neck was scratchy. I felt greasy under my clothes.

No one was using the waiting room. The mail hadn't come yet. I took off my coat and jacket and shirt in the little water closet and bathed myself from the sink and used the emergency electric razor I kept there to intimidate my whiskers. They didn't scare. I put on the same shirt and brushed the worst of the grit off the suit and combed my hair. I looked like a patched tire.

My answering service said no one had called. I got off the line quickly to have it open and relayed some room-temperature Scotch from the bottle I kept in the desk to a pony glass to my stomach. What it might do when it met up with the painkiller still in my system was of strangely little concern to me. I was having an out-of-body experience.

The sound of the mail slot clanking shut woke me. My watch read quarter to nine. The front of my head was pulsing independently of the rest of the skull when I got up and went over and bent down to pick up the mail.

It wasn't the mail. It was a thick brown envelope, hand delivered, slightly longer and wider than legal size, with the name of the consultancy firm I had called the day before printed on it. I took it over to the desk and sat down and slid a thumb under the flap. The telephone rang. I jumped on it. "Mozo?"

"Tomaso Acardo." The gentle accent was more pronounced over the wire. "Francisco asked me to call. He says he doesn't trust himself to talk to you this morning."

"I'm expecting an important call."

"So I gathered. You had a disappointing night. And a costly one for my nephew."

"I don't remember a lot of talk about guarantees."

"Cut the fucking tea party, Uncle Goat." I recognized Frank Acardo's voice in the background. "Ask him what he's got that was worth losing two of my best men."

"Francisco says—"

"I heard. Tell him the wheels are still turning. I'll call him when they stop."

Tomaso started to pass it on. His nephew cut him off. "You tell that fucking peeper he don't show up here by nightfall carrying Sam Mozo's head by the hair I'll feed him his balls."

"Francisco says—"

"I heard that too," I said. "Tell him me and my balls will be in touch." He was laughing gently in his deep rumble when I cradled the receiver.

The computer printout from the consultancy firm echoed what Mary Ann Thaler had told me about the motel on Tireman. It, the Park-a-Lot Garage, and half a dozen other parking facilities in the metropolitan area belonged to something called SouthAmCo, principal stockholder Manuel Anuncio Malviento. It went on to list the company's other holdings, including three auto dealerships and a substantial amount of property in Detroit, zoned residential. The most recent purchase had been made just that week. The telephone caught me digesting the information.

"Hombre, you owe me a Korean."

"You said yourself that hand-to-hand stuff was out of date," I said. "If it means anything, your boy Felipe took out an Acardo button."

"One dead lady friend, that's what you bought yourself, chamaco."

The receiver creaked in my hand. I leveled my voice. "I don't think so. Because if you killed her I'd go to the cops with the tape."

"Maybe you did already. I got people at Receiving. That's a pretty lady cop visited you this morning."

"There'd be a warrant out for you if I did."

He gave me a Spanish lesson. I listened, but this time I couldn't hear echoes. Well, he wouldn't use the garage a second time.

"It cost you," he said, remembering his English. "You be ready to move. *Now*. Felipe, he's parked across the street from your building. You ain' out front alone in fi' minutes, go back inside and wait for the mail. Her head be in it."

"How do I know she's still wearing it?"

"You don't, man." Click.

The gray Lincoln was standing at the opposite curb with its motor running when I came out carrying something in a small paper sack. The hood was dented in front and some teeth were missing from the grille, but aside from that Flynn appeared to have sustained all the damage from that collision. I looked for John Alderdyce's Japanese bug on my way across the street. I didn't see it.

I opened the front door on the passenger's side and got in. The upholstery hadn't been replaced yet and I was sitting on the knife-slash. Sam Mozo was hard on cars.

Felipe was wearing the same powder-blue suit under a black coat with a fur collar and a black tie and Oxfords. Up close his face was pockmarked but hardly less aristo-cratic for that. The concave hairline lengthened his already funereal features behind black wraparound sunglasses. His shoulder harness was fastened and as he spun the wheel to leave the curb, some extra material pouched under his right arm. If you know what to look for you can always tell when the tailor has left room for a holster. I pointed my chin at it. "That the thirty-eight you used on her wind-shield?"

He said nothing. It was warm in the car and I unbut-toned my overcoat. I smelled Brut. I didn't figure it be-longed to Felipe.

"Must be interesting working for Little Caesar," I tried again.

"He is my cousin."

"You're all cousins. Everybody must be related to every-body else down there."

"It is why I left." He twirled the wheel again. We were entering the southbound John Lodge now.

"You came up first?"

"Yes."

"Tough spot."

"Not so bad." He had decided to talk. "I get the job driving the car. Back home I drive the taxi: 'You want to see how the coffee is made, mister? I take you to the plan-tation, you get the free cup of the coffee.' *Chocho*. The money is much better here. In a year I send for Manolo, Sam Mozo you call him. Now for him I drive the car. America is funny."

"I laugh all the time. Did you drive Jackie Acardo from the beergarden to the motel?"

His face, which had become animated, fell back into its grave mode. He made no reply. That told me a lot. I dipped my line deeper.

"Good clean hit," I said. "To look at the room now you wouldn't know anything happened in it. There's something to be said for owning the roof you do your killing under. Too bad Mozo didn't pay as much attention to his help. He should have known about Charm's camera setup."

"There is no loyalty here."

I jumped on it. "You picked up Jackie at Joy and Evergreen and drove him to the motel for the hit?"

"Manolo said he wanted to talk to him. I just drive."

I sat back and let some scenery pass. "I guess it's a short step from driving a man to his death to running one over."

"I want to drive around you and the other," he said.

"Why didn't you?"

"Manolo he don't let me. His hand is on the wheel, his foot it is on the pedal on top of mine. The man is dead, I guess."

"You're a good guesser. Also a murderer."

He stopped at the light on East Jefferson. The shadow of the Renaissance Center darkened his features, or maybe it wasn't that.

"Who killed Charm, Ang or your cousin?"

The light changed. We stayed on Jefferson, following the river. The downtown skyscrapers rolled away behind us. I checked the mirror on my side for John's car. Nothing. Felipe turned down the heater. "None of us killed Charm," he said then.

I said, "I know."

22

He didn't ask how I knew, or even show interest. I wasn't in a mood to volunteer anything — not yet, anyway. I settled myself in for a long quiet drive, but on the edge of Gabriel Richard Park he turned again and we headed directly toward the river.

Long before it was renamed for Douglas MacArthur, the Belle Isle bridge had posed a temptation for local barnstorming pilots, beginning in 1913 with William E. Scripps, who later took on more daring journalistic stunts as publisher of the Detroit *News*. The water looks closer than it is and it's in the nature of fliers to pass under things and panic the flightless down below. Barely two lanes wide, the bridge describes a pistol-straight path out to a narrow stretch of water-locked real estate that was used to raise pigs a safe distance away from marauding wolves in the eighteenth and early nineteenth centuries, until Pontiac's warriors massacred a family there during the Battle of Bloody Run. The deadly race riot of 1943 started in a nightclub there and spilled over onto shore. Old Hog Island now boasts a park, a card casino, a children's zoo, the Detroit Symphony Orchestra, a fountain, various museums and conservatories, and a prettier name. On this day it was a snowfield with the water slate-colored around it and flashing in the sun.

Watching the mirror as we came off the bridge, I saw a flash higher up at the other end. It could have been a car, or a patch of ice catching the light. I didn't see it again.

We might have been alone on the island. There are more desirable places to be in February with the temperature in the twenties and winds skidding across from Canada whittling it down another ten degrees. When you're in the company of Colombian gangsters there is just no contest.

We parked in the lot and Felipe got out, signaling me to stay put. He walked around the car and opened my door. He had his gun out now — it was a short-barreled .38 Colt — and kept it tight against his left hip while he patted me down from my collarbone to my ankles and felt around inside my coat and jacket. He inspected my hat too, but when he reached for the drugstore sack next to me on the seat I caught his wrist.

"When I see Iris," I said.

The wind lifted the feathery hairs that still clung to his scalp. He paid it no attention. "How I know you don't have a gun in there?"

"You don't, man."

He stood chewing the inside of one cheek. He glanced down at a square gold watch strapped to his wrist. After a moment he stepped back, gesturing with the Colt. I got out carrying the sack. The cold wind slapped my face, stinging my cheeks like an open palm. I tugged down my hat and buttoned up. He gestured again and I started ahead of him along the footpath that divides the island.

The wind was a little less bitter there, cut off by naked trees on either side. The path was swept bare of snow but the earth was iron-hard and the cold was numbing. Before we had gone fifty yards my toes felt like rolled coins inside the thin leather of my shoes. If the warm-blooded Colombian was suffering he didn't show it, remaining ten paces behind me without comment or any change in his gait. I assumed he was still carrying the gun. If I had turned to look, my eyes would have strayed past him and maybe tipped him that John was following. *If* John was following. I felt all alone on that frozen rock.

Felipe grunted. I had gone past the path that branches off the main walkway toward the side facing Windsor. He had stopped short of it. I took advantage of the turn to shoot a quick glance behind him. Nobody.

The softball diamond was in the middle of a big clearing, snow-covered and bleak with the foreign city strung out gray behind it on the other side of the Fleming Channel. Three people were standing at home plate with their hands in the pockets of their overcoats. I saw Sam Mozo's big white hat and I recognized Iris' tan coat.

From the outfield I couldn't tell who the third party was. But I had an idea.

I had stopped. Felipe grunted again — he was making up for all the talking he had done earlier — and I continued across the clearing. The snow came up over the tops of my shoes and wedged itself in around my feet. I couldn't feel them at all now. Thoughts of frostbite glimmered through my brain, and of life without toes. But life of any kind looked good.

"Playing shallow, chamaco."

The wind warped Mozo's words and flapped our coattails. I held up at second base. Felipe was a presence behind me and to my right. Shortstop.

"Iris?"

"I'm all right." She sounded cold and tired. She was hatless and the wind had blown apart her hairdo. She whipped it out of her face. "That man last night—"

"Dead," I said. "It was part of his work. How you doing, Lester?"

Lester Hamilton said nothing. He had traded the motel's red blazer finally for a leather bomber jacket and pulled a cloth cap down over his eyes. The ends of the green-and-white-striped scarf were tucked inside the jacket. His face was lumpy and swollen.

Mozo said, "Lester knows what's good for him. I like a man knows what's good for him. Maybe I give him a job when this is finish."

"Who worked him over, the Korean?"

"I told him be gentle. Dead men know shit when you ask them questions. You ain' surprised to see him?"

"Here maybe. With you no. He had to have been the one who told you I was in Charm's office after he was stabbed. Lester was the only one who knew."

Lester shifted his weight agitatedly. "I kept our deal. I didn't tell the cops nothing."

"Of course you didn't. You had a lot more to gain by keeping it than the fifty I gave you. If the cops came to me and I told them Mozo was involved and they started digging, they might have found out about the tape. Only you couldn't know then that I'd never heard of Mozo."

"No more talking, chamaco. You got the tape?"

I patted the bag.

"Felipe."

Felipe took a step forward, but I put out a hand. He hesitated. I looked at Iris.

"There never was a strange license plate number on that list," I said. "No prowler broke into your room. Mozo put that drawing in your jewelry box himself. Being the owner of the motel he'd have a passkey."

It took her a moment to understand. "Then who stole the list? Who killed Charm?"

Mozo called out to his cousin again, sharply this time.

"Stay cool," I told Felipe. "Pardon the expression. You're clear. Neither of you killed Charm, just like you said. Why bother, for a list that even if it had Mozo's plate on it wouldn't be considered suspicious, because he owned the place? He certainly wouldn't kill him on account of the blackmail, because if Charm was smart enough to run his own little peephole racket without the boss's knowledge and accidentally videotape the boss killing Jackie Acardo in the privacy of his own motel, he must also have been smart enough to take precautions. He would see to it that the tape would be delivered to the authorities in case of his death or disappearance. Or at least he would tell the man he was blackmailing that he had seen to it. And yet all the time the tape was in the safe in his office. It was a dumb bluff, sure. After all, he was dumb enough to undersell himself. Five thousand wasn't that much more than he soaked any of his married victims who couldn't keep it in their pants."

"What you saying, chamaco?"

"It's a stall." Lester's tufted chin was out. "He ain't got no tape."

I looked at Mozo. My eyes were watering in the wind. "Killing Jackie Acardo and smuggling out his body brought down a lot of heat, from the cops and the Acardos. You didn't want to kill anyone else until things simmered down. So you went on paying Charm and even when your ex-wife came back to town, the ex-wife who could testify that she married you only so you could stay in the country, you didn't try to kill her, although there were plenty of opportunities. You tried scaring her, but she doesn't spook easy. Threatening notes didn't do it. Bulletholes in her car didn't do it. I'm not sure what you had in mind when you stole her unicorn pin right out of her room at Mary M's. Maybe you were going to send it to her by way of showing how easy she was to get to."

"Listen to the man talk." But he didn't stop me.

"A thing like that would appeal to you. I know from

experience you like to give demonstrations. Whatever the gimmick was, Charm's murder gave you a better one. Leaving the pin at the scene wouldn't lead the cops to Iris. It wouldn't be traceable. If it was you wouldn't have done it, because leading the cops to her would be the last thing you wanted. But it might get written up and broadcast, and she'd find out about it and know you play hardball. It might have been enough to send her back to the island."

"You Anglos always talking yourself into corners. You just said I don' kill Charm."

"That's right, you didn't. Lester did."

23

Lester shifted his weight again. He looked at Mozo, then at me, and that order said more than he was ever likely to. "Crazy," he said. "I got nothing against Charm."

I said, "The ground's full of people nobody had anything against. They didn't all die from natural causes. You told Mozo later that I'd been in the office ahead of him, and you took a beating for not telling him earlier. That took guts, because it was a lie. I found Iris' pin next to the body and Mozo had to have left it. There was no reason you'd have it. It's a good bet he'd have it on him, having gotten it from her room just that day while Iris was in my office telling me about the threats against her. You probably told him I jimmied the safe and took out the tape while you were busy calling the cops from the lobby."

Mozo's head turned on Lester. The big hat shadowed the Colombian's face and I couldn't read his expression. I continued.

"The way I figure it, Charm told Mozo the tape was with his lawyer or something. Mozo believed him—hell, it makes sense—or he'd have torn the office apart looking for it when he had the chance. You knew about the tape, Lester, or at least you knew about Charm's blackmail operation.

All you had to do was blunder into any linen closet in the building and see the setup. It must have looked like a sweet spot to a guy who wrote down license plate numbers for a living. You were an employee, he had no reason not to let you get close enough to stick a knife in his heart."

"You said yourself it was a pro done it. All I ever done was boost some wheels." He had put some distance between himself and Mozo.

"And got arrested for it. The slam's full of killers turned teachers. I'd forgotten that. You didn't, though. You re-membered your lessons. Safe-cracking would have been one of them. Office safes usually aren't much anyway, and anyone who's found his way around an automobile lock has a foundation to work from. Maybe there was just the one tape inside; probably there were several. You took them all out and stashed them somewhere to gloat over later. Then you called the boss. Not Andrew Gordenier, who was fronting for Mozo, because motel scuttlebutt would have seen through that a long time ago. You played dumb when he came, which couldn't have been easy. A potato with one eye is smarter than Mozo."

"Watch that mouth, chamaco. You still on the hook."

Lester had all my attention. His hands were out of his pockets now and balled at his sides. He had the river at his back and no place to run. Iris took her hair out of her face to look at him.

"Mozo had removed one body from that building al-ready," I said, "and anyway it wasn't his murder. He left the pin on an inspiration and told you to give him time to get clear and establish an alibi. He probably thought one of Charm's other victims was the murderer.

"Maybe you were hoping he'd cover it up. You had to know Mozo was into something other than the motel busi-ness. In any case you didn't waste time moping over it, because you had an ace. Me. Did I make you nervous,

Lester? Did you kill him when you did because I'd been snooping around and you were afraid I'd take the lid off the midnight movie factory before you could move in on it?"

"It's your story." I barely heard him.

"If you were afraid, you got over it. Now you were glad I was there to sic the cops on in case they leaned too hard on you because of your record. So you tore off that list of numbers I was after and got rid of it and called me. It would look like whoever killed Charm did it to get the list and cover up his part in the break-in in Iris' room. I didn't tell you that part, but motel gossip is always looking for fresh material, and the desk clerk had seen me going head-to-head with Charm. You'd have heard about it. That fifty I paid you to keep me and my client out of it must have handed you a laugh. If the cops came back on you, you could always tell them about that and make the whole thing so complicated they'd run out of taxpayers' money before they got it untangled. Time and money, that's what keeps most cases from being solved.

"You couldn't lose. If Mozo killed me over a tape I didn't have, it would be worth every bruise you took from Ang to have the heat off you. Then when everything cooled down you could start tapping the boss for real money. By then you'd looked at the tapes and knew what you had.

"You shouldn't have taken the list, Lester," I said. "That was one nail too many. But then you couldn't know that Mozo was the burglar, and that he wouldn't cross the street to get that list because he owned the place and he had every right to park his car there. As soon as I found out the motel was his I knew you were the killer. You were the only one who knew I was interested in the list."

My face felt stiff. Everyone's ears were red, but no one was paying attention to the cold now. Lester turned slightly, obscuring his right fist with his body. Mozo didn't see it. He was turning his face back to me.

"Chamaco, he got the tape, what you got in the bag?"

Lester's fist came around then and the sun caught something bright in it. He lunged across Iris, straight at Mozo. But the little Colombian was faster than he looked and the knife snatched only alpaca as Mozo backpedaled. He set himself and unlimbered a shiny pistol as long as his thigh from his own deep pocket. While all this was happening, something exploded not far from my right ear and Lester, who had spun to flee Mozo's weapon, turned the rest of the way around and fell, almost knocking Iris down.

I was moving too, tearing the Smith & Wesson out of the paper sack and swinging into firing position just as Felipe brought the smoking Colt around in my direction. He hesitated, then made up his mind. He was too late. I shot him in the chest. He jerked, looked down at the wound, looked at me, looked sad, and dropped onto his face. He was still holding the gun.

Two out.

Iris screamed — rage, not fear — and I whirled and saw her grappling with Mozo across Lester's body. He had his free hand on her throat, defending himself really, and she was clawing at his face with both hands, her knee in his groin. The big shiny gun came up. I took aim at him — and didn't fire. They were too close together for a revolver shot. I lowered it and started sprinting.

It was no good. My coat hobbled my legs. I unbuttoned it as I ran. I could hear my feet pounding the earth but I couldn't feel the impacts. If I stumbled. My heart was banging. Bile burned in my throat. To hell with if I stumbled; there was no chance either way. At 180 feet I was going to be out at home plate.

Sam Mozo snapped board straight suddenly. I was close

enough to hear the air roaring out of his lungs and I saw him go back on his heels with a hole in the front of his coat. He went on toppling backward, his eyes and mouth comic circles in his pie-tin face, the big gun cartwheeling and flashing in the sun. Then I heard the shot, a deep heavy bark that echoed off both banks of the river and died somewhere in Canada with a noise like waves slapping a wooden hull. Mozo squirmed on the ground, then relaxed slowly. Iris stood looking down at him. Her claws were still out. She lowered her arms.

The side was retired.

Passing the pitcher's mound, I slowed to a lope. I felt warm now — overheated, in fact. Sensation was tingling back into my extremities. My throat was raw. Sweat stung the stitches on my forehead. Iris became aware of me then and glanced down at the Smith & Wesson in my hand. I shook my head; I had no wind left for talking.

Her gaze went beyond me then. When I turned, John Alderdyce was walking out of left field from the ring of trees, carrying his deer rifle. The scope glinted.

24

He bent down over Felipe, holding his own head upright as he did so as if to keep fluid from spilling out. Then he straightened, and now he was moving a little faster. He was still in no hurry. He had on regular shoes and a lined raincoat that couldn't have been warm enough in that wind, but as he approached the batter's box he was sweating. He hadn't been near a razor in days.

"That one has a pulse." He rested the rifle's walnut stock on his shoulder with a hand on the barrel. "What about these two?"

Mozo was lying on his back with his coat buttoned and his arms spread slightly at his sides. His hat had slid down over his face and the front of the coat was stained. I lifted the hat. There was no meeting that gaze. I wasn't so sure about Lester, sprawled on his chest with legs tangled and his head turned to one side with the cap still jammed on it. I pried the jackknife out of his fingers, tossed it aside, and felt for the big artery on his neck. I couldn't find it. I plucked some fibers from my coat and held them under his nostrils, shielding them from the wind with my body. They seemed to stir. I told John.

He dangled his keys. "There's a radio in my heap. It's

parked next to the Lincoln. Get a wagon here — no, make it two, I forgot about the corpse — and take the lady home. I'll catch a ride."

After a second I took the keys. "How much did you hear?"

"Just enough, with the statement you're going to give me later. If one of these lives we may not need it. Either way we'll find out where this Lester flopped and maybe turn that tape."

"His last name's Hamilton. Someone at the motel should know his address." I breathed some air. "You sound like a cop."

"Vacation's over, I guess."

"I never spotted you."

"That was the idea."

I touched Iris' arm and she collapsed against me; it was all catching up. I got an arm around her. She was heavier than she looked. "Hell of a shot."

John grinned. It hurt him and he stopped. "I never could've made it stone sober. Who was it said he saw two balls coming at him and just swung between them?"

"Mickey Mantle," I said. "He hit a home run."

We shook hands.

The Japanese car was easy to figure out, once I'd identified the pictures on the dash. I strapped Iris in to keep her from sliding to the floor and radioed EMS. With her hair undone and her make-up streaked she looked like a little girl who had fallen asleep at her mother's dressing table. I took off her cork-soled shoes and spent some time rubbing circulation back into her feet. They were as cold as marble. Then I shook the snow out of my own shoes and put them back on. I turned on the heater and let it blow at our feet.

Halfway across the bridge she started to revive. "Take me back to Mary M's," she said. "Wake me up at Easter."

"We'll pick up your clothes there and go back to my place."

That brought her alert. "I'm getting married."

"Shucks. I was hoping you wouldn't remember that until I'd torn your clothes off and outraged you. When this story breaks you could fall down at Mary M's and break your head just like Jonesy. You're a witness."

"To what? There's nobody left to be a witness against."

"Wrong."

We were turning onto Jefferson. Two ambulances passed us and slowed for the turn, strobes flashing, sirens moaning. Iris looked at me, then at the street ahead. She asked no questions.

After a minute she took over the rearview mirror and used a fistful of Kleenexes from the box in the glove compartment to remove what she could of her smeared make-up. Then she borrowed my comb and took the tangles out of her hair. Finally she knotted it behind her neck. She looked like Nefertiti in the monsoon season. I asked her where she spent last night.

"At Felipe's house in Sterling Heights. His wife was there, and two little kids. None of them spoke English. The kids bunked on the living room floor and I got to sleep in a bed with Miami Vice sheets."

"Anything else?"

"Well, I got raped, but that was about it."

I turned onto Woodward and waited for a streetcar to cross in front of us.

"Mozo?"

"The little spick wasn't any better at it than he was the first time."

"He hurt you?"

"He didn't have to. When a man's got you he's got you. It isn't like I had anything to fight for."

She sounded tired. I crossed the tracks behind the streetcar. "Mary Ann Thaler wins the pool," I said.

"What?"

"Nothing. Mozo made a clean sweep of the police department, that's all."

"Are you mad at me?"

"Not at you. Never at you."

The salt they had spread on St. Antoine had done its work. Melted ice stood in brown puddles, axle-high in spots. I made sure Iris wouldn't be stepping into one when I parked, and got out to open the door for her. She was already on the sidewalk when I made it around the car.

Sara answered the door, wearing a fuzzy pink angora sweater and blue jeans. I wondered if she ever wore shoes. When she saw me she smiled. "Hi." Then she saw Iris. "Hey, you okay? We thought—"

"Where's Mary?" I asked.

"She's in the basement. What happened to your head?"

"Years of disappointment. Can we talk to her?"

"Sure. I'll show you the stairs."

The basement was well-lit, paneled, and freshly concreted. It contained a Nautilus machine and an exercise bench and assorted weights. Mary M, in sweatsuit and sneakers, lowered the dumbbell she was curling when we entered. Her face was shiny.

"Iris! Did they—"

"I'm in one piece," she said. "Was anybody hurt?"

"Jonesy was taken to the hospital. How did you get loose?"

I said, "She got loose. That's the main thing, right?"

"Right." She set the dumbbell down on the exercise bench. Then she opened her arms and took a step toward Iris.

"Stay back!" I blocked the way.

Mary stopped. The skin of her face tightened, obliterating the lines.

"Amos?" asked Iris.

I took my hand out of my coat pocket with the Smith & Wesson in it. "Imitate a statue," I told Mary. "I'm not Jonesy. I know what you are."

"I don't—" said Mary.

"Sure you do. Flynn said it. You wouldn't know him; you were only an accomplice before the fact in his murder. He said Jonesy wasn't one to let somebody he'd never seen walk up to him and kick him in the head, much less a Korean who'd just finished breaking in the front door. At the very least he wouldn't be taken with his gun still holstered under his arm. It would be someone he might expect to have standing in front of him sometime or other. Someone like the owner, or who he thought was the owner. A woman who just happened to be proficient in karate.

"She'd be talking to him, maybe telling him for the umpteenth time he wasn't welcome here—by then he probably wouldn't even hear it anymore—and then she'd move and he'd be on the floor bleeding. Maybe she'd have put something in one of his ham sandwiches just in case he was quicker than he looked, which he was if he was anything like Flynn. There'd be plenty of stuff in a house full of reformed prostitutes, some of them junkies. Then while he was out cold she'd open the door for Mozo and whoever was with him, Felipe or Ang or both, to come in and carry Iris off. They must have caught her sleeping, or she'd have put up a better fight."

"They did," said Iris. "I dozed off in the chair. I woke up with chloroform in my face."

"You'd have been wide awake if anyone had broken through the front door. I checked the lock on my way out. It was a dead bolt and it was intact."

"You're the one who got hit too hard in the head." Iris was becoming shrill. She was still reacting from the morning. "Mary's my friend. This house and her guests mean more to her than anyone or anything. Why would she help Mozo?"

"Because this house and her guests mean more to her than anyone or anything. Right, Mary?"

"You did your homework." Her wiry little body was coiled and there was a trapped brightness in her eyes. She had never looked more like a rodent.

"I found out this morning. Mozo's corporation, SouthAmCo, bought up your lease the day Iris arrived. It was cheaper to acquire the place and mix it in with the company's other holdings than it would have been to mount an offensive and risk bringing in the cops. Iris has been a tagged animal ever since she came back to town. At the garage, in the motel — who recommended the motel?" I asked Iris.

"The attendant." She sounded subdued. "He said I'd get a discounted rate if I told the clerk I'd garaged my car at the Park-a-Lot. He said it was a nice place. I could use the savings."

"Raleigh looked like a charmer. My guess is he told you all that when he came down with the car. After he'd talked to Mozo in the office and shown him your signature."

"Maybe. I don't remember."

"Probably. Point is wherever you went he had a leash on you. No wonder he was in no hurry to kill you."

"Mary stole my pin?"

"It was a small thing against losing her lease and turning her broken doves out into the cold. But once you've done it, going up to assault and complicity in kidnaping isn't such a big leap."

Mary looked less hunted. "Please believe me, Iris, it wasn't anything against you. He said he'd throw everybody out and doze the place and build a parking garage. There are more parking garages in this town than cars. You know how many places there are like this? Not one. Where would they all go?"

"A man died," Iris said.

"Men are what filled this house to begin with. Anyway, I had nothing to do with that."

I said, "The law might not agree, after they've read my statement and confirmed the ownership of this house."

She flipped the exercise bench up easily. With the dumbbell at my end there was no trick to it. I stepped back quickly and got an arm up to deflect it and she yelled and spun and kicked the gun out of my hand. Then she lost her balance and fell. Iris had caught the dumbbell with a foot as it rolled and given it a shove, striking the ankle Mary M had been supporting herself on. She twisted in midair and landed in an animal crouch. I scooped the gun up off the floor and rolled back the hammer. She relaxed.

"Call the cops," I told Iris.

"No. Let's just leave."

"She'll run."

"Where'll she go?"

I looked at Mary M. She was sobbing now, sitting cross-legged on the floor with her face in her hands, her shoulders working. "What's going to happen to them?" she said. "What's going to happen to them?" I elevated the barrel and let the hammer down.

"What about your clothes?"

"I'll buy new ones. Please, Amos, let's just go."

We went. I could hear the sobbing from upstairs.

The snow heaped in front of my driveway had set in rusty clods. I guided the Chevy through the ruts and parked it in the garage. We sat there for a long time after I killed the engine.

"Mary was as tough as anyone," she said.

"That's the scary part."

"I trusted her ahead of everybody. Including you."

"She used to be a prostitute. That doesn't mean anything except maybe she confused selling her body with selling herself and then it didn't seem so hard."

"I was one, don't forget."

"Only by profession." I got out. This time she let me open her door.

We went in through the kitchen. Being with her I was aware of the lifeless smell of the air in a house in winter where only one person lives. In the living room she looked around.

"Place needs plants."

"Just keeping myself alive is work enough," I said. "Can I get you something? I think there's a tea bag somewhere."

"Right now really cheap whiskey sounds great."

"You should listen to my liquor cabinet. The bathroom's in there." I went into the kitchen.

The shower was running when I came out carrying two full glasses on a tray and set them down on the coffee table. I carried mine into the bedroom and peeled everything off down to the skin. I put on black woolen slacks and moccasins and a sweater and finished my drink and bought a refill in the kitchen. The bathroom door opened and closed. In the living room she had on two towels and her glass in her hand.

I'd forgotten the smooth brown of her shoulders and legs and the perfection of her feet. The towel on her head emphasized the Nile look, and with the rest of the make-up scrubbed off she seemed younger, almost adolescent. Not quite, though.

She saw me looking. "I had to get out of those clothes.

There's a robe in there but I could turn around inside it. I could put it on anyway."

"Not if you're comfortable."

"All I took out of Mary M's was my pin. I was damned if I was going to let her keep that."

"I'll get you something to wear and then you can go shopping."

"Charles will wire me money. I hate asking him."

"I'll make you a loan."

"I'd hate that more."

I grinned at that. There wasn't any reason to. She smiled back, and there wasn't any reason for that either. We were leering at each other like two kids who had run away from home and found ourselves alone in a motel room and now we didn't know what we were supposed to do.

She drank. "My father?"

I stopped grinning. "I found George Favor."

"Where?" She almost spilled her whiskey. She set the glass down on the scratched coffee table. "Is he alive?"

"He's alive. Where doesn't matter."

"Doesn't matter? I've been looking—"

"Get some rest. I'll take you to your father later. You'll want to be fresh when you talk to him. Also clothed."

"I don't know if I could sleep knowing—my God." She put a palm to her cheek and smiled again and looked away. "I'm starting to feel like a little girl whose daddy's been gone a long time. What did you bring me, Daddy? God, what'll I say to him? How does he look?"

"Don't work yourself up to something that won't happen. It isn't like he dandled you on his knee and warned you to steer clear of boys who use Vaseline on their hair. A long time ago he met a woman; you were the result. That's all. It will be clumsy. There won't be any violins."

"I know that."

"You say it, and maybe you think you do. Everyone's

looking for where he came from and some of us find it. Then what? It never changes anything. You buried your parents. Everything else is just a biological accident."

"Why are you angry?"

"I'm not. Hell, yes, I am. The harder you look for a thing the more disappointed you're going to be when you find it. It's never as big or as bright or as sweet as what you've got pictured. Half the time it's so small and dull and bland you trip over it looking for it before you realize you've found it. Why shouldn't I be angry?"

We were standing close. She put her arms around me and squeezed tight, holding on for a long time. She smelled of soap and Iris. Then she leaned back against my supporting arm and looked up at me. Her eyes were dry.

"Explorer Scout," she said. "Knowing the things I've done for money and the things I did with the money, and still trying to keep me from getting hurt. You're sweet and stupid."

She closed her eyes and I kissed her. After another long time I swatted her on the rump.

"Sleep. If the telephone rings, let it. It'll probably be the cops wondering why I'm not downtown dictating my statement."

"Amos—"

"Don't finish it," I said. "You might want to take it back later."

25

The snowman in Westland looked lonely. The kids who had built it were in school and the sun had melted it and the cold had refrozen it, giving it a glaze like the seat of a worn pair of pants. It had a drunken list and its charcoal-briquette eyes were shedding black tears.

Nothing about the house next door had changed. The brick was still yellow, the wood around the windows lead-colored where the paint had curled away, the windows curtained and dark. My footprints from the day before yesterday were still there without company, swollen and crusty, with some later snow hammocked inside them. I followed them around to the trailer in back.

No more snow had been removed from the walk since my first visit. The shovel stood where Sweet Joe Wooding had left it. You could stand in that one spot and believe the earth never turned. It was a definite temptation.

I mounted the wooden steps, knocked, waited, and went inside. I was alone with the furniture and the smell of old marijuana. I walked over to the heavy curtain and pulled it aside. It masked a single unmade bed with a dented pillow and white sheets gone dirty ivory. A white clay ashtray on the cracked bedstand contained a roach in a clip. I touched a finger to the burnt end. Cold. I tapped on a folding louvered screen in the corner, then craned my neck around the end. The tub and toilet were unoccupied.

Back outside I smoked a cigarette and looked at the house. There were no tracks leading to it, but a crust had formed on top of the snow and a slight person could walk on top of it without leaving any. Not being slight I made some footprints of my own and tried the back door. It was unlocked.

It led into a mudroom without plaster or insulation. The black rubber mat was wet, but condensation could have been responsible for that. I opened an inner door and rancid air hit me in the face.

This room had a window, but the curtains were drawn. I found the light switch and used it. No lights came on. I pushed aside one of the curtains with a rattling of plastic rings and sunlight fell on a white stove and refrigerator and sink and a sheet-metal table with a moldy plate on it and mouse droppings in the plate.

The living room was just as dark until I drew aside a curtain there and looked at some uncovered furniture with a skin of dust on it and framed posters on the wall. I lifted a corner of the sheet on the only covered object in the room. It was a gray leather trombone case with brass hinges. I replaced the sheet.

Some of the posters were all text, advertising performances in circus lettering. The latest date was October 3, 1963. Others had pictures. These were photographs and paintings of a good-looking young black man with a neon grin and straightened black hair worn in a high pompadour, who looked a lot like Nat King Cole. In several of them he sat straddling a bass viol with his fingers poised on the frets. One was a black-and-white snapshot mounted at an angle on a blue field with red lettering:

In Person

JOSEPHUS "SWEET JOE" WOODING

Boss Bass

Maharajah of the Moth-Box

Templar of Tailgate

The World's Most Versatile Jazz Musician

The photograph was a profile of the same young man playing a slide trombone.

I found the color snapshot Iris had given me in my breast pocket and compared them. I didn't need to. I'd known they would match before I set foot in the place. "One note looks pretty much like all the others on the sheet," George Favor had said. Especially when the note didn't match the name.

Joe Wooding had a reputation for violating union rules. It would be a career habit with someone who had started playing long before musicians' unions grew teeth. The love of music was too strong in him to be chained by regulations. His membership had been suspended several times, narrowing his employment options, but being a professional he would find a way around that, appearing in places whose management didn't care or borrowing a friend's union card and playing under his name. Being a virtuoso on the bass, piano, and trombone, he'd have no trouble carrying off the pose so long as he didn't meet anyone who knew him or knew the man whose card he was using. Kingston, Jamaica, would be a good place not to be seen by acquaintances of Joe Wooding or Little Georgie Favor. The band he had recruited and brought with him certainly wouldn't say anything that might blow a gig.

In a place like that he could continue the act offstage without fear of discovery. He could pitch a fling with a local singer and then leave when the run ended and she would never know that the father of her child wasn't who he said he was. It would explain why Iris' father never got in touch with her; any attempt her mother might have made to reach George Favor would have been ignored by him, never having been in Jamaica and being clinically sterile, as another attempt to extort child support, and Wooding wouldn't have known he had a daughter until he was old and sick and in no condition to acknowledge her.

But a man who had shut up his house to keep the memories inside when his wife left him wouldn't remain untouched by a visit from the daughter he didn't know existed, however he might deflect her from the ravaged and dying thing no one recognized as the spruce young blade in a thirty-year-old photograph. A thing like that would move him. I passed through a square arch and down a short dark hall lined with autographed pictures in glass frames and stood in an open doorway near the end.

The curtains weren't quite shut, allowing a crack of light into a bedroom that had been shared by two people before it became stale and dark and without character. The air inside had a familiar bitter smell, strong not because it was fresh, but because it had been shut in for days, maybe since the day I had visited. On a bureau stood a photograph in a dusty frame of an older Wooding with his arm around a woman twenty years his junior. They were smiling, and his expression, while not as dazzling, was a link between the flashy young jazzman who had posed similarly with Iris' mother and the thing on the double bed.

He lay atop the covers, looking smaller than before in a suit that had been far too large for him for months, but that had been brushed and arranged with the care of a mortician preparing for his own services. Inside the suit was a shell shriveled by age and cancer, everything but the big head with its block features and nose that had been flattened in some long-ago backstage scuffle. He had combed his thin hair and trimmed the slim dark moustache and touched them up with something that was now definitely black dye, for it had an unnatural sheen against dead flesh. His eyes were glittering half-moons in the dim light. One of the sockets had filled with something dark that had spidered down from a puckered hole in his right temple and dried there. The big Ruger lay on the covers, its butt resting in his open right palm where it had come to rest.

I didn't see a note. He wouldn't have left one. The condition of his body would tell the medical examiner as much as he would want anyone to know. I didn't go inside the room to see if I was wrong about the note or to feel the clamminess of his skin or the stiffness of his flesh. Instead I drew the door shut gently and went back the way I had come. The snowman next door was still weeping when I pulled away from the curb.

26

In late January a female ticket agent at Detroit Metropolitan Airport had reported finding a conical object inside a stall in the women's room. The terminal had been evacuated while a bomb crew checked it out. It turned out to be a Thermos bottle left behind by a plumber, but reaction was still setting in almost a month later and Security was trashing the Bill of Rights all over the place. As a non-passenger I wasn't allowed beyond the checkpoint.

"It's all right," Iris said. "I'd rather wait alone. It'll be my first chance to sit down with my thoughts."

She had on a red beret in place of the yellow one she'd left at Mary M's and the tan coat and new boots. A couple of male passengers and a gray-haired pilot looked her over on their way to the metal detector. I said, "I'll cut through what red tape I can on this end. The air cargo outfits don't like shipping bodies. You never see caskets in their TV ads."

"Charles' old partner will see to that. Charles said he caught him just before he checked out of his hotel in France."

"Not every fiancé would go his future father-in-law's transportation and burial. That may be a new one."

"So I know two special men." She watched the female

guard going through an old lady's purse. "I'm still not sure Joe wouldn't rather stay here. Am I being selfish?"

"It's not supposed to matter where your remains wind up. Anyway, a cemetery in Jamaica beats a trench on Wayne County property. He rented his house and the trailer wasn't worth anything." I handed her the flight bag full of new clothes.

"I want to bring him flowers without having to go through this. Maybe it's guilt. I can't even remember what I said to him when I left his trailer that one time. How could I not know my own father?"

"Easy. You'd never met him. I didn't place him and I'm supposed to be trained to know what to look for. You were after George Favor. You had no reason to take a second look at Joe Wooding."

"Why didn't he tell me?"

"It was too late to matter. By then he'd probably already made up his mind to kill himself before the cancer did," I lied.

She was watching me now, not buying any of it. "Charles makes a good living — "

"I get by. I was spinning my wheels when I bumped into you and got a break from missing wives and runaways and insurance work. I thought I was burned out until I saw John Alderdyce. He's on his way back now too. He'll have relapses, but the important thing is he's bottomed out. Maybe helping him turn around did something for me too, points in purgatory or something. Getting paid besides would be overkill."

"I'll write."

"I'll read what you write."

She kissed me hard. Then she turned away and put her bag on the conveyor and stepped through the detector. The last time I saw her she was turning heads on her way down the terminal, carrying the bag.

It was days before I found the unicorn pin she'd stuck in my pocket.

The bucket seat on the passenger's side of the Chevy was tilted as she had left it when she took her bag out of the back. I looked at it, feeling empty, and tipped it back and started the engine. The announcer on the radio said we were headed for an early thaw. Icicles were dripping from the lamps along the Edsel Ford and residents in St. Clair Shores and the Grosse Pointes were being warned that the lake was rising. We were entering the first of the series of false springs that would continue through April.

I'd called Detroit Receiving Hospital that morning and a nurse had told me that Felipe Salazar, Sam Mozo's cousin, was expected to recover following surgery to remove a bullet from his chest. In the same tone she informed me that Lester Hamilton had died in Emergency without having regained consciousness. After that I'd tried John Alderdyce at police headquarters, but he was out and I asked for Mary Ann Thaler, who said they were still looking for the videotape Lester had killed Eldon Charm to get. She couldn't talk long. The Colombian drug dealers had started killing one another over Sam Mozo's territory and the entire department was involved in throwing water on the fire.

Approaching the lot down the street from my building I passed a black Camaro parked at the curb with two men seated in front. I got a better look at them on foot, at their brown Latin faces and the way they held their cigarettes high between their index and middle fingers like Gilbert Roland. They elaborately paid me no attention at all as I walked past the car and went inside. On the stairs I transferred my gun from my overcoat pocket to its holster.

The key met no resistance when I inserted it in the lock on my inner office door. I got the gun out again and backed up a step.

"Cut the drama," somebody said inside. "Nobody's laying for you today."

I recognized the voice. I pushed the door open. Frank Acardo was sitting behind my desk. He had on a vicuña coat with peaked lapels over a gray suit and a silver tie with black diamonds on it. A pearl felt hat with a braided band lay in state on the blotter. His face looked like the corner of a building with eyes.

"No wonder you can't afford a better lock, the hours you keep."

Both his hands were in sight on top of the desk. I holstered the Smith & Wesson. "Where's Tomaso?"

"Taking the dog for a leak. Nobody else to do it until Jonesy finds his feet, and anyway he likes the little mange. They're two of a kind; no balls."

"Maybe."

"Maybe means what?"

"Just that I'm making conversation."

"You look like you could stand some time in the hay yourself," he said.

"Nice of you to care."

"That's civilization for you, saying you give a shit when you don't. You really work here?"

"When I'm not wasting time talking to cheap gangsters."

"Cheap, yeah. That's the word I was looking for. You broke our deal, Walker. You were going to hand me something on Mozo I could take to the board and get the green light to pencil him out. Nobody said nothing about dragging in the cops."

I stretched my legs from the customer's chair. It was a tight fit in my overcoat. I shook out a Winston and tapped it against the pack. "You never know which way these things are going to jump," I said. "Anyway, Mozo's dead. That's what you wanted."

"The shit killed my old man. I wanted to blow him off myself. No buttons, just me and a piece and that little spick looking at me over the barrel."

"The board wouldn't approve."

"Bunch of slits, my old man called them. And he sat on it. But I didn't come here to talk about the board."

"You could've fooled me."

"No, I don't think I could. I underestimated you, pal. I won't make that mistake again."

He waited for me to ask. I lit the cigarette and pulled over the souvenir ashtray from Traverse City and blew smoke and said nothing. He gave up waiting.

"Flynn was a good soldier, one of the best. That deal we made cost plenty when I lost him. But I'm not bitching. Don't you want to know why I'm not bitching?"

"You tapped the state lottery for a million."

"A million, I spit on a million." He leaned over and spat on my rug, which was a contradiction I didn't bother to point out. "No, I'm not bitching on account of right now I'm farting rose petals. I'm farting rose petals on account of since Mozo got it every little Juan Valdez in town is tripping over his tacos to grab what Mozo left behind and hitting every other little Juan Valdez in town to do it. Meanwhile Jackie Acardo's boy isn't letting any grass grow, if you get my drift. This keeps up we'll have our old lock back on the town by Easter. The spicks had their day. Now it's the guineas' turn back at the trough."

His Richard Widmark was getting to me. "You came here to tell me that?"

"I thought you might like to know you're off the stick. I'm still out one button, maybe two if Jonesy don't come out of Receiving with all his jacks, and maybe you owe me and I'll be in a position to collect someday. But because it all turned out so good I won't be putting any hurt on you. Maybe that's worth knowing."

———

192

"Tomaso could have told me that himself. It sounds like his idea in the first place."

"Uncle Goat never did have all *his* jacks. But he's got a heart in him as big as his ass and he asked me to stop by and tell you to your face you're off the stick. I'm feeling so good I say, sure, what the hell? Make an old man happy. Maybe he'll put in a word when he sees God."

"You're smart to cover your bet."

He watched me. "Well, I guess I didn't come here to get thanked."

"Maybe I do owe you," I said.

"Yeah?" He had started to get up.

"Tomaso told me he had twenty quarries. Your grandfather gave him his first but you don't run that into a string unless you've got brains and not a little ruthlessness. He said you were a hothead and had to be watched to see you didn't draw too much fire. I think he'd do anything to prevent that, even if it meant dealing with the enemy. He's got his own business to protect."

"You saying he'd turn?"

"I don't think he'd see it as turning. I know if he went down it wouldn't be for something he had no control over."

"You got him mixed up with someone with guts."

"Maybe. He likes that dog. He said it would win the fights it cared to."

"I got no time for this." He stood and put on his hat.

I shrugged. If they won't be warned you can't make them. "You're always welcome here, Frank. Next time call. If I'd known you were coming I'd have installed bars in the windows."

"That's Mr. Acardo, fuck."

"Interesting name. Is that hyphenated?"

His little eyes grew sunken. On his way around the desk he stopped and looked down at me. The skin on his ugly face was pulled back tight. "I see you again I'll feed you to the dog."

I tapped some ash into the tray and took another drag. He waited again, but I didn't say anything again and he went out. I didn't tell him about the Colombians. He would have said he had no time for it.

The noises came a couple of minutes later, three of them very fast. It might have been someone clapping his hands. After that the sound of the Camaro taking off was shrill but remote, like Spanish laughter.